The soldier quickly glanced inside the buggy. "You haven't got traveling bags with you, so I take it you don't plan to stay long."

"That's right. Just today."

"I'd caution you not to return after dark. There's no telling who you might run into on these back roads."

From the corner of her eye Peg shot a quick glance at the soldier with the beard, who was still looking at the reticule. *Union Army or not, I'd hate to run into this one anywhere!* Peg thought.

"You may proceed," the sergeant said.

Miss Hennessey smiled again, picked up the reins, and clucked to the horse. The soldiers rode past them with a great clatter, stirring up clouds of dust that caused Peg to cough.

The moment they were out of hearing Peg asked, "Why did you say that I was your daughter?"

"Not now." Miss Hennessey's voice was low and quick.

"What do you mean, not now? I—"

"Hush!"

To Peg's amazement Miss Hennessey pulled a small handgun from her reticule and tucked it on the seat under her skirt. In a low voice she said, "Whatever may happen next, don't be afraid."

ALSO AVAILABLE BY JOAN LOWERY NIXON
IN LAUREL-LEAF BOOKS:

LAND OF DREAMS
LAND OF HOPE
LAND OF PROMISE
A CANDIDATE FOR MURDER
THE DARK AND DEADLY POOL
THE GHOSTS OF NOW
THE KIDNAPPING OF CHRISTINA LATTIMORE
THE NAME OF THE GAME WAS MURDER
THE OTHER SIDE OF DARK
SHADOWMAKER

The Orphan Train Adventures

Keeping Secrets

Joan Lowery Nixon

Published by
Bantam Doubleday Dell Books for Young Readers
a division of
Bantam Doubleday Dell Publishing Group, Inc.
1540 Broadway
New York, New York 10036

The trademark Laurel-Leaf Library® is registered in the U.S. Patent and
Trademark Office.

The trademark Dell® is registered in the U.S. Patent and
Trademark Office.

ISBN: 0-440-21992-2

RL: 5.8

Reprinted by arrangement with Delacorte Press

Printed in the United States of America

March 1996

10 9 8 7 6 5 4 3 2 1

OPM

For Katherine Joan McGowan
with my love.

A Note From the Author

During the years from 1854 to 1929, the Children's Aid Society, founded by Charles Loring Brace, sent more than 100,000 children on orphan trains from the slums of New York City to new homes in the West. This placing-out program was so successful that other groups, such as the New York Foundling Hospital, followed the example.

The Orphan Train Adventures were inspired by the true stories of these children; but the characters in the series, their adventures, and the dates of their arrival are entirely fictional. We chose St. Joseph, Missouri, between the years 1860 and 1880 as our setting in order to place our characters in one of the most exciting periods of American history. As for the historical figures who enter these stories—they very well could have been at the places described at the proper times to touch the lives of the children who came west on the orphan trains.

Joan Lowery Nixon

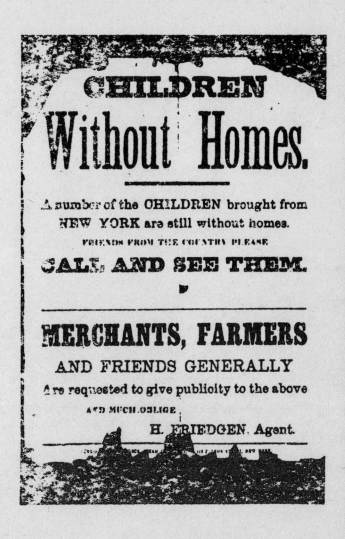

CHILDREN
Without Homes.

A number of the CHILDREN brought from
NEW YORK are still without homes.
FRIENDS FROM THE COUNTRY PLEASE
CALL AND SEE THEM.

MERCHANTS, FARMERS
AND FRIENDS GENERALLY
Are requested to give publicity to the above
AND MUCH OBLIGE

H. FRIEDGEN, Agent.

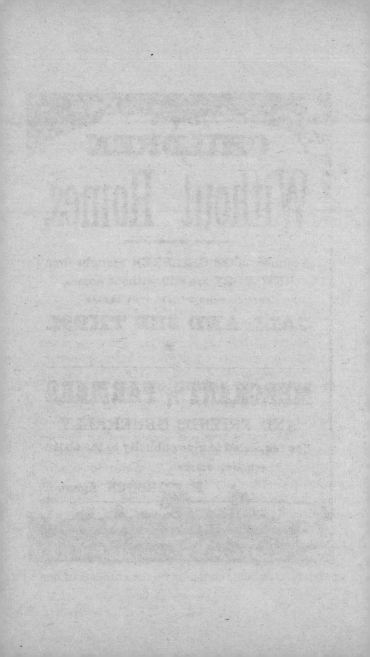

1

"FINISHED!" JENNIFER PUT the last dish away in the cupboard and quickly turned toward her grandmother. "You promised to read to us from Frances Mary's journal as soon as the kitchen was in order."

"It looks good to me," her brother, Jeff, said. Hoping that Grandma wasn't watching, he brushed a few stray toast crumbs from the kitchen counter into his hand and stuck his hand in the pocket of his jeans.

Grandma winked at Jeff. "The kitchen looks good to me too—especially that very clean counter." She held up the book, which was covered in faded blue fabric, and said, "I have the journal right here, so why don't we settle down on the screened porch, and read about the Kelly family's next adventure?"

Jennifer and Jeff raced to see who could get to the porch first. Jennifer curled up on the cushions of one of the wicker chairs and squirmed with anticipation as Grandma opened the book to Frances's delicate, spidery handwriting.

"Frances Mary dated this entry, 'Autumn of 1863,' " Grandma said.

"Was the Civil War over then?" Jeff asked.

"No," Grandma said. "The War Between the States had escalated. In January of 1863 President Abraham Lincoln signed the Emancipation Proclamation, freeing all slaves in Confederate states, and the bitterness and anger increased."

Surprised, Jeff said, "But that was two years after the war started. I thought that freeing the slaves was what the war was all about."

"Last year in history class Mr. Wilson told us that the main reason for the war was economic," Jennifer said. "The northern states wanted to put a stop to slavery in the United States, but the people in the southern states said their economy would collapse without slave labor. They seceded from the Union so they could form their own country, and they fired the first shots, which began the war."

Wishing that Jennifer weren't always such a know-it-all, Jeff grumbled, "Okay, okay. Let Grandma get started. I want to hear more of Frances's story."

"So do I," Jennifer said. She settled back as Grandma began to read:

No one who has not been touched by the devastation of war could possibly understand its horrors. With some commanders and their troops it is not enough to win a battle or lay claim to strategic areas. People like Confederate William Quantrill and his raiders seem to take great satisfaction in terrorizing entire villages by stealing, burning, and destroying homes and stores and—even worse—randomly killing all males who favor the Union, including young boys and elderly men.

During the fourth week of August we gave shelter to a badly frightened woman, who had escaped Quantrill's murderous sack of the town of Lawrence by fleeing northward. It was the mercy of Providence that led her to our quiet farm community and to our home. In spite of the kindness and reassurance shown her by the Cummingses, Violet Hennessey—for that was her name—was so shaken and fearful that for days she could not abide to be left alone.

"I cannot remain in Kansas," Violet told us. "I want to go home to Boston."

"Travel at this time will be very difficult," Mrs. Cummings told her, but Violet was insistent.

"I've heard there are still trains able to leave St. Joseph for the East," she said. She seemed intent— almost stubborn.

"St. Joseph, like all of Missouri, is in turmoil."

"But the area in and around St. Joseph has been spared the violent attacks from jayhawkers and bushwhackers that have plagued the counties along the border farther south. Frances, you told me yourself that your family members who live in and near St. Joseph have remained free from harm."

Violet's thoughtful, deliberate words were in vivid contrast to her ordinary manner. As soon as she had finished speaking, she pulled her shawl more tightly around her shoulders, her sad little face poking out like a wary swamp turtle's. "If I can get to St. Joseph," she said, "somehow, some-

*where, I'll find a safe place in which to stay until
I'm strong enough to travel."*

  A safe place in St. Joe.

  Immediately, I thought of Ma.

2

PEG KELLY CLOSED her eyes and inhaled the warm cinnamon-sugar smells of the kitchen. Nibbling, she held a tiny bite of apple dumpling on her tongue to make the birthday treat last longer.

Her mother smiled and winked. "You needn't be afraid to gobble it down. There'll be more dumplings with supper tonight."

Peg gulped and dipped her spoon into the flaky pastry for another bite. "You're a good cook, Ma."

"And you're a good daughter, little love."

"I am not little. I'm eleven now." Peg sat up defensively and squared her shoulders, as though she could will herself to add an inch or two to her height of four feet, eight inches. "I'm practically grown."

Noreen Kelly Murphy added wood to the fire in the cast iron cookstove, then picked up a heavy pan, which contained a fat hen, stuffed almost to bursting with a mixture of bread crumbs, minced onion, and herbs.

Peg's eyes gleamed. "Roast chicken, too! Oh, yum!" It wasn't often they were able to have meat. Both the Confederate and Union raiding parties helped themselves to farmers' stock and food supplies. There was precious little left for the stores to sell.

As Ma tucked the chicken inside the oven, Peg heard the creak of buggy wheels and the clop of horses' hooves stop in the road outside their house.

"Someone come to visit?" Ma asked and held aside the lacy curtain that hung over the kitchen window. "Oh, merciful heavens!" she cried in delight. "It's Frances Mary!"

Peg threw down her spoon and raced to the door, flinging it open and screeching, "Frances! Frances!" She wrapped herself in her big sister's hugs.

Frances turned to greet Ma, who held her tightly. Over Frances's laughter Ma chattered on. "It's been months since I've laid eyes on you, Frances Mary! And look at you! Blooming with good health, praise be! How is my Petey? Did you bring him with you this time? He's well, isn't he?" She craned her neck, staring toward the wagon.

"He's fine, Ma. I'm fine. And so are the Cummingses."

Ma abruptly stopped speaking. In surprise, Peg followed her mother's gaze and saw a woman standing beside the wagon. She was pale, her skin nearly matching the faded gray of her cotton dress and bonnet. Almost apologetically she hung back, and when she met Peg's glance, she smiled shyly and ducked her head.

Frances, one arm still around her mother, turned

toward the woman. "Ma, . . . Peg," she said, "I want you to meet Violet Hennessey. Miss Hennessey fled from her home in Lawrence, when Quantrill and his raiders burned the town. She needs a place to stay for a short while, Ma, so I brought her to you."

"And rightly so," Ma said without hesitation. She immediately took charge, sending Peg to plump the pillows on the bed in the spare room and fill the pitcher with fresh water.

By the time Peg returned to the kitchen, Frances had left to stable the horse, and Ma had ushered Miss Hennessey into a chair by the fireplace.

A cup of tea already in her trembling hands, Miss Hennessey murmured, "It will be just for a few days. Just until I can find suitable lodgings."

"We're happy to have you stay with us," Ma reassured her. She pulled up a chair facing Miss Hennessey. "Here in St. Joe we heard about Quantrill's attack on Lawrence. It must have been terrifying."

Eager to hear any details that Miss Hennessey might offer, Peg took a step forward. She realized her mistake when Ma immediately spotted her.

"Miss Hennessey's two carpetbags are on the floor by the door," she said. "Will you please take them to her room, Peg, my girl? One at a time now, because they're heavy."

"But, Ma, I want to hear about the raid."

"Now, please," Ma said firmly.

To argue in front of a guest was unthinkable, so Peg silently turned and did as she had been told, but inside she fumed. *She sent me off on purpose so I wouldn't hear. She treats me as if I'm a child. And I'm not! I'm close to becoming a full-grown woman!*

The first bag wasn't particularly heavy, but Peg lugged the second bag up the stairs with difficulty. It was more scuffed than the first one, the flocking worn and stained at the corners. *How did Miss Hennessey escape quickly if she had to carry these two bags?* Peg wondered, then shrugged.

By the time Peg returned to the kitchen Frances had joined Ma and Miss Hennessey, who was now spooning up a bowl of chicken broth.

Peg glanced wistfully toward the apple dumpling she had left. Her mouth watered for it, but it would be rude to eat it if Miss Hennessey had not been served some, and she would rather wait than give up any of her own portion at the moment.

"And your friend, Johnny?" Ma was asking Frances. "Is he also well?"

Frances's cheeks suddenly turned pink, and she stared down at her cup of tea. "He writes when he can," she said. "He's with the Kansas Volunteers."

"He's in my prayers, love, along with all the other young men who have gone off to fight." Ma patted Frances's shoulder.

"On the Union side," Peg said and pulled up a chair.

"On *both* sides," Ma corrected.

"Ma!" Peg was shocked. "You can't pray for the Confederates!"

"I'm praying for all the boys who have left their homes to fight for what they believe in, no matter if they're right or wrong," Ma said. "They all have mothers who lie awake at night worrying about them."

"But we're under martial law. The provost marshal arrests anyone who helps the enemy in any way."

Ma laughed. "Fortunately, the provost marshal has no way of knowing what's in my mind and heart."

Frances smiled and reached over to hug Peg. "Let

Ma be," she said. "Today's your birthday, and I didn't forget. I brought you a bag of molasses taffy."

"Yum!" Peg said, but at that moment Miss Hennessey gave a little moan and swayed in her chair.

Ma and Frances jumped to their feet, Ma clutching Miss Hennessey's shoulders to keep her from falling.

"I'm sorry." Miss Hennessey's voice was so faint she could scarcely be heard. "Maybe it was the long journey. I'm so tired . . . so tired."

"Then it's bed for you," Ma said. "A good sleep may be all that you need. Don't even think of coming down to supper. I'll bring up a tray."

"Thank you," Miss Hennessey whispered. With Ma's help she rose from her chair and stumbled from the room, supported by both Ma and Frances.

Quick as a shot Peg snatched her half-eaten apple dumpling and began to gobble it down. It was no longer warm, and the cream had soaked through the lower crust, but it was still delicious.

In a few minutes Ma and Frances came downstairs, pausing at the foot of the staircase to talk in low tones.

Peg felt a lump in her throat as she watched her sister, whose dark, shining hair gleamed in a beam of late afternoon sunlight that came from the fanlight window over the front door. Frances had grown taller and even more beautiful. With her small waist and rounded breasts and hips, at sixteen she had become a lovely woman.

Peg slid her hands over her own flat chest and grimaced. She wanted to look like Frances, to be as kind and loving as Frances, and to be as brave as Frances had been when she risked her life to work with the Underground Railroad, helping slaves to escape to freedom.

Besides, she thought, as she licked the last drop of

cream from her bowl, *by the time I'm sixteen maybe Ma will stop treating me like a child!*

Supper preparations soon began, and Peg helped by cutting pole beans into a pot for boiling and setting the table.

Her stepfather, John Murphy, arrived home from his blacksmith's shop. The shirt that stretched over his broad shoulders was stained with sweat. He greeted Frances warmly and raised his thick black eyebrows in surprise when told of their guest.

"Were you acquainted with this woman before the raid?" he asked Frances.

"No," she answered.

"Then how did she happen to go to the Cummingses for help?"

"Pure fortune," Frances said. "She was on the road after dark and spotted the lights in our house. She knocked on our door and asked us to take her in."

"Who are her people? Where is she from?"

"That I can't tell you. I simply know that Miss Hennessey is frightened and alone. She wanted to leave Kansas, and I thought that Ma . . ."

"Your ma. Ah, yes indeed," Mr. Murphy said with a frown. "She's very good at taking in strays, without thinking of the consequences. Just between you and us and no one else, last week Noreen risked arrest by feeding a Union Army deserter who stopped and asked for food."

Indignant, Ma thrust both hands onto her hips. "It's not up to me to be judge and jury, John Murphy. All I saw was a frightened, hungry boy—of no more than sixteen years of age, if that much—curled up under the washtub in our backyard, trying to get some sleep as he traveled homeward."

John smiled and put an arm around Ma's waist,

drawing her close. At one time Peg, still missing the father she had lost, had resented John's open affection for Ma, but no longer. Over and over she saw that he sincerely loved Ma and was a good husband to her, and it was obvious that Ma loved him.

"Tell me more about this Miss Hennessey," John said to Frances. "I heard that the raid took the entire town by surprise. How did she manage to escape the raiders?"

"A merchant with a horse and wagon was fleeing Lawrence. He agreed to let her ride with him."

"That's not very fast transportation. A Reb on horseback could catch up with a wagon in less than a minute."

"They were ahead of the Rebs," Frances explained. "Violet left Lawrence from the north as the raiders entered the town from the south."

"Interesting," he said. "How did she learn they were coming?"

Frances grew flustered. "I don't know, and she was so upset that we didn't bother her with questions. I suppose that people fleeing ahead of the raiders brought the news."

"John!" Ma broke in. "Stop ragging Frances. She brought Miss Hennessey here as an act of kindness because the poor woman was so frightened. You get so curious that you shake a bit of news to pieces the way a dog worries a bone."

John shook his head sadly. "It's Quantrill I'd like to be shaking. The Lawrence raid was a terrible act of revenge on that evil man's part. Word has it that Quantrill led his raiders shouting, 'Kill! Kill!' The man must be mad."

John's news didn't surprise Peg. Marcus Hurd, who was undoubtedly the dirtiest, meanest boy in school, was nevertheless a good source of information. One day before class, Marcus had told them in gory detail what he'd heard about the collapse of the makeshift prison in Kansas City, in which many of the wives and women friends of Quantrill's men had been killed or badly wounded. Quantrill had vowed to get even.

"Vinny Ottman came by today to get his horse shod," John said. "The poor man was broken. It seems his cousin Frank was caught by a Union patrol, accused of spying for the Confederates and hanged on the nearest tree."

"Oh, dear," Ma said. "I'll go pay a call on Vinny and Jane."

"Why did they hang him on the nearest tree?" Peg asked. "Why didn't they take him to jail?"

"There's no quarter given to spies, my girl," Mr. Murphy said. "On both sides, if a spy is caught, he's immediately hanged."

With a concerned eye on Peg, Ma pulled away from her husband. "Enough of all this talk of war," she said. "The chicken is browned, the potatoes are baked, and it's time to celebrate Peg's birthday with her favorite supper."

The meal was every bit as delicious as Peg knew it would be. Afterward, Ma prepared a tray, taking it to Miss Hennessey herself, and Frances insisted on doing all the cleaning up.

Peg curled contentedly into a chair by the fire Mr. Murphy had laid in the wide, brick fireplace in the parlor. This was not only a special day for Peg, there was a guest in the house, so the parlor would be readied for her use. How different from their usual routine of spending the evening at the kitchen table, Peg thought. Most evenings she'd be busy with schoolwork, Ma would have a lap full of mending, and John would go over every inch of *The St. Joseph Gazette*, bits and pieces of which he'd read aloud.

As Peg stretched like a cat, sucking on a piece of the taffy Frances had brought her and luxuriating in the warmth from the fire, Ma came downstairs with a report that Miss Hennessey had eaten every bite of her supper and had settled back in bed, ready once again to sleep.

"The color's come back into her face," Ma said with satisfaction as she placed her oil lamp on the table. "With rest and good food she'll be herself in no time at all."

Her gaze went from the small clock on the parlor table to Peg. "It's getting late. Time for bed, love," she said.

"Ma!" Peg complained. "I'm older now. I shouldn't have to go to bed at eight-thirty. Besides, it's my birthday!"

"Birthday or no birthday, you have school tomorrow," Ma replied. "I'm not sending you off to Miss Thomas to yawn in her face and stumble over your sums." She bent to kiss Peg on the forehead and pull her to her feet. "Good night, love."

"Ma, you don't treat me seriously," Peg complained. "I'm old enough to take on a fair share of the cooking and cleaning—and do a good job of it! Yet you send me off to bed as though I'm an infant! You're all going to talk about Miss Hennessey and the raid and her escape, and I want to hear, too!"

"No, you don't," Ma said. "Things have happened in this miserable war that are too horrible for young ears to hear and young minds to comprehend."

"But—"

"Good night, Peggy, my love," Ma said. Her hug turned into a gentle push toward the stairs.

13

Grumbling under her breath, Peg hurried outside through the cool night air to the privy, then—taking one of the lamps—slowly climbed the stairs to her room, which was across from the head of the stairs. She poured cold water from the pitcher into the basin and washed her face, then slipped into her nightgown and slid under the puffy quilt, pulling it up to her chin.

The bed was soon cozy with body warmth, and the distant hum of voices from the parlor made Peg drowsy. She closed her eyes, snuggled under the quilt, and began to drift into sleep; but she was suddenly startled awake by the creak of floorboards in the hall outside her room.

3

THE FAINT CREAKING stopped. Whoever had trod on the boards must still be there, neither moving on nor returning. Overcome with curiosity, Peg slipped out of bed, pulled on a cotton wrapper, and silently opened her bedroom door.

Deep in the shadows, hugging the wall on the top stair, sat Violet Hennessey, her chin stretched forward and her head tilted as if she were listening to the conversation in the parlor below.

Peg sucked in her breath, astounded at the change in Miss Hennessey. The shy, drab victim had disappeared, replaced by a handsome woman, her long, dark hair woven in a thick braid that hung over a ruffled and embroidered white cotton gown and wrapper more elegant than any Peg could have imagined.

The tiny sound Peg had made alerted Miss Hennessey, who whirled, eyes wide. For just an instant they stared at each other, then Miss Hennessey's shoulders curled inward and she slumped against the wall, tugging the neck of her wrapper into a wad under her chin. A tiny, apologetic smile flickered on her lips and she motioned to Peg to come closer.

Blinking, Peg wondered if she had imagined the quick glimpse of the woman she thought she had seen. She dropped to the top stair beside Miss Hennessey, who whispered into Peg's ear, "I left my reticule somewhere downstairs. I was on my way to retrieve it but was suddenly overcome with dizziness. I sat down, afraid I'd fall."

"I'll get Ma," Peg said and began to rise, but Miss Hennessey clutched Peg's arm with fragile, trembling fingers.

"Please don't worry your mother with my condition," she murmured. "I'm feeling stronger now. I'm sure I can go back to my room unaided, but I do need the sleeping powders I keep in my reticule. Please, Peg, will you fetch it for me?"

Tears welled up in Miss Hennessey's eyes. She looked so pitiful that sympathy for her immediately swept away any doubts Peg may have had. "Of course I will," she said.

She helped Miss Hennessey to her feet and trotted down the stairs and into the parlor.

The conversation suddenly stopped.

"You were talking about Miss Hennessey, weren't you?" Peg demanded.

Frances looked surprised. "We were talking about Petey. I was telling them how well he's reading now and about some of the funny stories he makes up."

"It doesn't matter what we were talking about," Ma

16

said sternly. "Just what are you doing out of bed so long after your bedtime?"

Peg sighed elaborately and rolled her eyes. "Ma, you just take it for granted that I'm breaking rules. You don't even give me a chance to explain, even though I have a perfectly good reason for coming downstairs. You don't even *ask* why I'm here."

"That's exactly what I did do—ask," Ma told her. "And now will you please give us the answer?"

Indignantly, Peg stood as tall as she could. "Miss Hennessey left her reticule on a table. She asked me to get it for her."

Ma put down her mending, and got to her feet. "You're right, Peg. You did have a good reason. I'll help you find the reticule."

Frances jumped up. "I know where it is. It's on the table by the door," she said.

"I'll get it myself!" Peg whirled around, swept up the plain, black reticule and marched toward the stairs. When she realized that Ma was right on her heels she stopped and turned. "Miss Hennessey asked me not to bother you," she said. "She won't like it if you come upstairs."

"She may need something," Ma answered. "Fresh water or an extra blanket."

"If she does, I can take care of it," Peg complained. "I know how to fetch water or find a blanket."

Ma put her hands on Peg's shoulders. For an instant she hesitated. Then she said, "Don't be so quick to imagine offense, love. You're a fine, capable girl, and I appreciate all that you do. Give us a kiss now, and I'll see you bright and early in the morning."

Her resentment dissolving in a rush, Peg kissed her mother's cheek and hurried up the stairs.

She dutifully offered the fresh water and extra

blanket to Miss Hennessey, who huddled in the middle of the bed, the quilt pulled up to her nose.

"No, thank you," Miss Hennessey mumbled. "I need nothing more than rest."

Peg, more sleepy than she'd want to admit, gratefully shut the door to the guest room behind her and headed for her own bed.

In the morning she reluctantly prepared for school, begging Ma, "Can't I at least stay until Frances gets the horse and wagon?"

When Ma shook her head, Peg turned to Frances. "Why can't you visit with us longer? Do you have to go so soon?"

"I'm needed at home," Frances said, and Peg saw Ma wince.

"This is your home, too," Peg insisted.

Frances glanced at Ma and smiled, then gently smoothed the curly, red fringe of hair that hung over Peg's forehead. "I'm teaching school now, Peg. I was lucky to find a full-time position nearby, and I don't want to lose it."

"Teaching school? Oh, Frances! I wish you were my teacher!"

"No, you don't," Frances teased. "I'd make you stay after school and clean all the slates."

"Who's teaching your students while you're here?"

"Mrs. Cummings was kind enough to step in for me for a few days, but I can't impose on her good nature."

Peg sighed in admiration of her big sister. Sixteen, and already with a full-time teaching job! There had been times lately when Peg—hating the daily memorization of arithmetic tables and history dates—had promised herself never to set foot inside a schoolhouse, once she had reached fourteen. But at the moment she began thinking favorably of someday becoming a teacher, just like Frances.

As Ma packed a small lunch pail for Peg and a large basket of food for Frances, with treats inside to take to Petey, she worried aloud.

"Are you sure you'll be safe traveling alone?" she asked.

"I'll be fine, Ma. I can take care of myself."

"But what if Quantrill and his like . . . ?"

"Quantrill and his men ran to the south when Union forces rode into Lawrence."

"There are other bushwhackers about."

"Ma, you know as well as I do that it's the lower counties along the Kansas-Missouri border that have had most of the trouble. During the last few months there've been very few skirmishes in Buchanan County or in northern Kansas."

"All well and good, but you'll be traveling until late tonight."

Frances smiled. "I can handle a rifle as well as any man. I'll be safe. I promise."

A rifle! Was there nothing Frances couldn't do? Peg's heart swelled with admiration.

Ma paused, folding a cloth over the contents of the basket. She looked at Frances with such yearning in her eyes that the feeling in Peg's heart turned to a dull ache. "Then I ask God's blessing upon you, Frances Mary. May he send His angels to guide and protect you on your journey."

She took a long, shuddering breath and added, "My goodness! Look at the time! Run, Peg, or you'll be late for school."

"Ma!" Peg complained, but she gave her mother and Frances quick hugs and hurried toward the front door.

Peg had no sooner shut the front door behind her when Miss Hennessey, well swathed in shawls, suddenly appeared at her side. Peg jumped and let out a squeak of fright.

"Oh, dear, oh, dear! I didn't mean to startle you," Miss Hennessey said. She gripped Peg's arm with much more strength than she'd shown the night before. Bending close to Peg's ear she said, "I've been waiting to talk to you. I need your help."

"I'll get Ma," Peg began, motioning toward the house, but Miss Hennessey shook her head.

"This is something just between you and me." Again the shy smile flickered. "It's easy to see that you're an intelligent, brave girl. Brave and smart enough to keep a secret."

"What secret?"

"That I'm staying here at your home."

Peg knew she must look surprised, because Miss Hennessey hurried to explain. "Oh, there are bound to be some people who will know I'm here. I'm not in hiding from your neighbors. I'd just rather that as few people as possible know of my presence. I'm asking you not to tell your friends, or your teacher, or the shopkeeper, or anyone else with whom you might stop and visit."

Peg hesitated. The only thing that could possibly pull her away from Frances Mary's departure and this mysterious woman who had come to visit them was to tell her friends what had happened. May would turn pink with envy, and her sister, April, would beg to be told more. Marcus and Willie would scoff, but they'd listen, especially if Peg made the story as exciting as possible. She'd already planned how she'd begin. "It was late at night. We heard a frantic pounding at our door . . ."

"After my dreadful experience I'm so afraid." Miss Hennessey, tears rushing again to her eyes, interrupted Peg's thoughts. "I'm so terribly, terribly afraid."

"I won't tell," Peg promised, disgusted at her quick capitulation, because she always kept her promises, no matter what. There went her few moments of glory at school.

"Thank you," Miss Hennessey whispered. She patted Peg's shoulder, then silently opened the door and slipped into the house.

Why should Miss Hennessey be so afraid? Peg wondered. She'd left Lawrence before Quantrill had even arrived. He and his men certainly wouldn't follow her here.

Peg heard the school bell in the distance. She was going to be late, which meant she'd be punished again. What was it going to be this time? A slap on the hands with a ruler? Or sitting in the corner during recess?

Taking a firm grip on her lunch pail and books, Peg ran as fast as she could up the hill.

Close to four o'clock, when Peg arrived home, she found Ma and Miss Hennessey in the kitchen having a companionable cup of tea. Ma greeted Peg with a kiss, took the cozy off the large teapot, and poured Peg a cup.

Miss Hennessey's eyes searched Peg's face, and Peg—knowing what she was asking—gave a slight nod.

Gratefully, Miss Hennessey sank back into her chair, cradling her cup under her chin, breathing in the fragrant steam.

"You'll be glad to know that Miss Hennessey is feeling nearly her own self again," Ma told Peg.

"That's good news," Peg said. Miss Hennessey still

looked dowdy and plain, but her cheeks were pink, and she did seem stronger. For one thing, she was no longer ducking her head, peering upward like a frightened kitten.

As Peg stirred sugar into her teacup, Ma asked, "Tell us about school, love. What did you do today?"

"Nothing," Peg said and took a sip, wincing as the tea burned her tongue.

"Ah, it's amazing to me how much learning you absorb, sitting there in the schoolhouse day after day doing nothing at all."

"Oh, Ma," Peg mumbled. "You know what I mean. We just don't do anything interesting enough to talk about."

Miss Hennessey spoke up. "Your mother and I were talking about her children and the homes they live in." She reached across to gently touch Noreen's hand. "It must have been very hard for you to give them up."

"It would have been much harder to be unable to give them a decent life if they'd remained in New York City."

"And if Mike—" Peg stopped abruptly, hiding her embarrassment in taking another sip of the hot tea. Ma probably hadn't told Miss Hennessey about Mike being arrested in New York City for copper stealing and how she saved him from being sent to Tombs Prison by appealing to the Reverend Charles Brace of the Children's Aid Society to intercede with the judge.

"Frances told me about Mike," Miss Hennessey said softly, as though she could read Peg's mind. "Your mother was a very brave woman. And you children . . . you were very brave, too, to come west on an orphan train."

Brave? Peg hadn't really thought about being brave. Going to foster homes was something that had to be done, so they did it without question. She remembered how frightened she'd been at the room filled with strange people who'd come to look them over, and how she'd clung to Danny, wondering if they'd find homes . . . wondering if they'd be separated. That journey had taken place three long years ago, before Ma had been able to come west to join them.

John Murphy, whom Ma had married, made a fairly comfortable living with his busy blacksmith shop—and continued to do so in spite of the war—but it wasn't good enough to support six children, so all the Kelly children but Peg—Frances and Petey with her, Megan, Mike and Danny—had stayed with the kind and loving people who had taken them in.

"Now that you've heard about our family, why don't you tell us something about yours?" Ma asked Miss Hennessey. "Were you staying with family in Lawrence?"

"No. I stayed only briefly in Lawrence and not with family. My family is from Boston," Miss Hennessey said into her teacup.

"Are they still there?"

"No. Not any longer." Her voice so faint Peg could scarcely hear her, Miss Hennessey said, "It's all too fresh, too painful to talk about."

"I'm sorry," Ma said. She glanced at the clock, jumped to her feet, and busied herself with scraping carrots at the drainboard. As an afterthought she looked over her shoulder toward Peg. "Best get to your sums, my little love."

"I will, Ma," Peg answered, unable to completely hide her aggravation at being reminded.

Miss Hennessey smiled at Peg. "I'm sure you're very good at your studies."

"Fairly good, I guess," Peg answered modestly.

"I could tell. I know you must do well in all your subjects. Do you like history?"

"Not really," Peg admitted. "I hate having to memorize names and dates."

Miss Hennessey nodded sympathetically. "I suppose that names and dates will always have to be memorized, but history should be interesting. History is about people and the fine things they've done and the mistakes they've made. History is a collection of exciting stories. Don't you agree?"

"I guess so," Peg answered. It hadn't occurred to her to think of history in those terms.

"For example, I know some interesting stories about the childhood and background of President Abraham Lincoln. Perhaps after supper tonight you might like to hear them."

"Yes. Thank you." Peg smiled at Miss Hennessey and reached for her schoolbooks. She was surprised at what a nice person Miss Hennessey had turned out to be. Maybe she had been wrong in having a few misgivings about her.

4

Over the next few days Violet Hennessey became not just a nice person in Peg's mind, but a friend.

Ma never failed to remind Peg of perfectly obvious things Peg had planned to do anyway: "It's breezy out, Peg, so take a shawl."

"Don't forget to tidy your room before you leave for school."

"Remember to study your spelling, love. Last week you lost out in the final round of the spelling bee because you misspelled the word Miss Thomas gave you."

But Miss Hennessey treated Peg as if she were another adult: "Your muffins are delicious. I would love to have the receipt."

"I've heard that President Lincoln is considering a proclamation that would create a national holiday of

Thanksgiving on the last Thursday in November. How do you feel about this, Peg? Do you think a holiday like this would be successfully observed—especially during this time of war?"

"Oh, Peg! I have a delicious story to share with you. Last spring that circus man, John P. Barnam's star attraction, General Tom Thumb, who is only thirty-five inches tall was married to Miss Lavinia Warren, who is a scant thirty-two inches tall! Well . . . a friend of mine who attended wrote at the time that the bride's dress was quite expensive but overly flounced and . . ."

Peg, who bridled at her mother's continual advice, luxuriated in feeling almost grown-up when she was with Miss Hennessey.

On the third day of Miss Hennessey's stay Ma, who felt that fresh air was important to good health, suggested that Peg take Miss Hennessey walking.

To Peg's surprise, Miss Hennessey seemed eager to walk, and as they left the house she said, "I understand there is a delightful overlook above the Missouri River. Could we walk there?"

"Oh, yes," Peg said. "There's a little woods, and a winding path and wildflowers in the spring. It's one of my favorite places."

Eagerly she led the way, but she was puzzled when Miss Hennessey's attention turned to the woods and not to the wide view of the river.

The next day, when Peg returned from school, Ma was alone in the kitchen.

Peg snatched a cold biscuit left over from breakfast, stuffed a large bite into her mouth, and asked, "Where's Miss Hennessey?"

"Out walking," Ma told her, "and don't talk with your mouth full."

"I'll catch up with her," Peg said and was through the door before Ma could answer.

She looked to the right and the left, but Miss Hennessey wasn't in sight. *The woods*, Peg thought, remembering Miss Hennessey's interest, and she hurried in that direction, taking a familiar shortcut through some unfenced property.

Although there was still no sign of Miss Hennessey, Peg entered the woods, shivering a little in the damp shade. The smell of decaying leaves underfoot tingled her nose, and she stopped to take a deep breath. The woods were silent, with not even the rustle of small animals or chirps of birds. Had she got here before Miss Hennessey?

From the corner of her eye Peg saw a sudden movement farther inside the thick grove of trees, and she ran toward it, the soft spongy floor of mulch swallowing the sound of her footsteps.

"Miss Hennessey?" she called, but stopped short as a man stepped from behind a tree and glared at her. He was beardless, with long, dark hair that curled to his shoulders; and he wore a butternut-colored shirt that looked much like a Western plainsman's coat. His right hand moved toward the pistol that was thrust into his belt and rested on the polished butt.

The man's shirt frightened Peg more than his revolver. Although many westerners wore this type of shirt, it was well known that Quantrill's guerrillas had adopted the design as a kind of special uniform that set them apart.

"But they're Confederates," Peg had said to John Murphy, who had shown her the drawing in the newspaper. "Why don't they wear the Confederate Army uniform?"

"They may call themselves a unit of the Confederate Army," he'd answered, "but they're nothing more than a bunch of lawless brigands. They'd never have been able to gain the power they hold if it weren't that so many of them are Missouri boys, protected and hidden out, when need be, by their families and friends."

The guerrilla spoke, breaking into Peg's thoughts. "What are you doing here?"

Peg was so frightened it was hard for her to speak. "I—I was l-looking for Miss Hennessey."

His gaze shot nervously to the left and the right. "Who's Miss Hennessey?"

Peg's stomach clutched as she realized she had told this man the name of her friend. She had to leave this place. She had to warn Miss Hennessey away.

"I'm going home," Peg said and took a step backward.

He shook his head and slid the pistol from his belt. "You're not going anywhere."

Off to one side Miss Hennessey suddenly stepped into view. "Put your gun away, sir. She's only a child," she said.

"Else . . . ," the man began, his eyes widening in surprise.

" 'Else what?" Miss Hennessey interrupted. "Don't threaten us, sir. We mean you no harm."

The man looked confused, but he did as Miss Hennessey had told him. He sucked in his stomach and slid his pistol under his leather belt.

"You're traveling, and you're hungry," she said. Her gaze was sharp as she stared at him. "You need food. Is that right?"

"Yes," he growled. He paused a moment, then scowled at Peg. "One of you will have to go for food. The other will stay with me."

"No!" Peg blurted out.

"It's all right, Peg." Miss Hennessey rested a hand on Peg's trembling arm. "He wants to make sure you'll return with the food and without informing any authorities."

"Me?"

"Yes. Get some food from home without attracting attention. Bring some bread and cheese. Your mother has some fall apples at hand."

Peg balked. "Come with me. I don't want to leave you here alone with him. He has a gun."

"He won't harm me. Go, please. Now."

Peg turned and ran through the edge of the woods, but she stopped, once outside the cluster of trees. Below the cliff the mud-colored Missouri river ran swiftly, eddying around the small craft that navigated against the flow. Pressing a hand against her chest, as if she could stop the frantic pounding of her heart, Peg tried to calm down and think.

The man was one of Quantrill's raiders. Peg was sure of it. Miss Hennessey had been very brave in sending Peg away and staying behind as a hostage, but it was obvious she didn't know this was one of Quantrill's men or she might have been frightened into one of her faints.

As Peg thought about the terrible deaths these bushwhackers caused—deaths of loyal Union men— her face flushed with a hot anger. The raider who was keeping Miss Hennessey hostage didn't deserve the food he demanded. He deserved only to be stopped and arrested. But it would take too long to go for help.

Peg knew these woods. She came here often with May to play hide-and-seek, then flop on the grass to watch the bustle of activity on the river landing below. If she cut around to the east and came up behind the raider . . . So frightened that her hands shook, Peg picked up a fist-sized rock and silently entered again the grove of trees. Could she stop him? Would she be able to?

"I *have* to," Peg whispered aloud.

She quietly slipped through the woods, sidling from tree to tree, until in the distance she could see the Reb, whose back was to her. He was tall, and his shoulders were broad, so at first she couldn't spot Miss Hennessey. More frightened than ever, Peg dropped to a crouch and worked her way behind some bushes to one side.

She gasped when she was finally able to get a good look at Miss Hennessey. She and the raider were standing close together, intently involved in a conversation Peg was too far away to hear.

Miss Hennessey laid a hand on the raider's arm, her fingers stroking his sleeve, and smiled up into his eyes. He bent toward her, but her hands slid to his shoulders, holding him off. "Go," she said, so plainly that Peg could read her lips. "Hurry."

The raider took a few steps, then turned and called back, "I should have word soon."

"I'll be ready," Miss Hennessey said.

Peg slid back behind the trunk of the nearest tree, afraid to breathe until the man had plenty of time to leave the area. But as she waited, her fear turned to anger. Miss Hennessey said she had run from Quantrill's raiders, yet here she was on very friendly terms with one of them.

She deceived me! Peg fumed. *She had planned to meet him here. Sending me for food was only a ruse to get me out of the way!* Peg slammed the stone to the ground and ran heedlessly into the woods where Miss Hennessey still stood—waiting for Peg to return with the food, no doubt.

"Everything's all right, Peg dear," Miss Hennessey called as soon as she spotted Peg. "He's gone." She looked from Peg's empty hands to her scowling face. "You didn't bring food," she murmured.

"No, I didn't. That man was one of Quantrill's raiders. I recognized the shirt." Accusingly, Peg added, "I couldn't leave you alone with him so I picked up a rock and cut through the woods from a different direction."

Miss Hennessey interrupted by hugging Peg so tightly it was hard enough to breathe, let alone talk. "You darling girl!" she cried. "You tried to save my life!"

Peg, still angry, struggled to free herself. "I didn't need to, did I? I saw the way you looked at him."

Miss Hennessey, a woebegone expression on her face, dropped her arms. "Now you realize why I have been reluctant to speak about my family, and why I was in Lawrence. James is my cousin. Until recently, he and his family lived near the Missouri-Kansas border in Independence. But poor James's father and uncle were tragically murdered, their home burned, and their property stolen by a Union patrol, simply because they refused to take sides against their neighbors and friends. James escaped and ran to join the bushwhackers, giving his allegiance to the Confederates. I came to find him, to beg him to reconsider, to remember our family's loyalty to the Union."

A tear rolled down her cheek, and she gave a little sob. "But my pleading did no good. James wouldn't listen."

Shocked at the story and embarrassed by her previous anger, Peg stammered, "Y-you planned to meet him here. How? When?"

Miss Hennessey pulled a cotton handkerchief from

her sleeve and pressed it against her eyes. "James sent word to me that Lawrence would be sacked. He told me to make my way to St. Joseph where he'd get in touch with me."

"How did he find you?"

"That doesn't matter."

"I heard him tell you that he'd soon have word, and you said you'd be ready. What did you mean?"

"This is a family matter, Peg. I can't explain everything to you. It's been difficult enough to tell you about James's defection to the Confederates."

"I'm just trying to understand," Peg said. "You told us that you were afraid of Quantrill's raiders."

"Oh, I am!" Miss Hennessey cried. "I am firmly convinced that Quantrill is mad, and his madness is infecting his men. I can see heartbreaking changes in my cousin. James was once a gentle, caring man, but alas . . ." She shuddered. "You can see how desperately I needed to meet with him, to try to get him to change his ways before he leaves with Quantrill and will be too far away for me to try to influence him. You do understand now, don't you, Peg?"

Peg thought a moment. If she had a relative who had become a bushwhacker, wouldn't she try to change him? If it were Mike? Or Danny? She'd tell only half-truths without thinking about it twice if she thought she could rescue them. Miss Hennessey hadn't exactly lied. All that she'd done was try to save her cousin. "I understand," Peg said.

Miss Hennessey hugged Peg again, this time gently. "Thank you," she whispered. As they drew apart she added, "I'm not asking you to keep things from your mother, Peg. I'm just asking you not to upset her."

Until Miss Hennessey had brought up the idea, Peg hadn't even thought of upsetting Ma. Once Ma heard the story, though—especially if Peg included picking up a rock and going back to defend Miss Hennessey against a man with a gun—she was bound to become upset.

"I would like to tell her in my own way," Miss Hennessey said.

Peg quickly nodded agreement. Miss Hennessey's version wasn't likely to include the episode with the rock.

Quietly they walked home. Peg scurried upstairs, leaving Ma and Miss Hennessey to talk over hot cups of tea. Twice she tiptoed to the head of the stairs and tried to listen to their conversation. There was a low murmur of voices, neither of them upset or angry, and a sniffle or two from Miss Hennessey, so Peg began to relax.

During the next two days Miss Hennessey was even more attentive to Peg. From one of her carpetbags she produced a copy of Charles Dickens's *A Tale of Two Cities* and read aloud with such expression that Ma— every bit as entranced as Peg—lost track of the time and forgot to remind Peg to go to bed.

Soon, both Ma and Miss Hennessey received letters. Ma tore hers open eagerly and joyfully read aloud that Frances had arrived at the Cummingses' home safely and that Petey had enjoyed his treats and begged her to take him next time she came to St. Joe. But Miss Hennessey clutched her letter and edged out of the kitchen, hurrying to her room to read it in private.

It was almost an hour later when she came downstairs. The kitchen was steamy with a soup bone and vegetables on the boil, and Peg brushed back the tendrils of damp hair that curled around her face.

Smiling shyly, Miss Hennessey said, "Noreen, dear,

it's time for me to take lodgings elsewhere. It would be unfair to continue to take advantage of your kind hospitality."

Although Miss Hennessey's shoulders hunched under the gray shawl she'd wrapped tightly around them, Peg saw a spark in her eyes and heard what seemed to be suppressed excitement in her voice. Peg gulped down the lump of disappointment that rose in her throat. She liked Miss Hennessey to be there and hated to see her leave.

Ma's eyes widened in surprise. "Where will you go, Violet?"

"I'll remain in St. Joseph for a short time," she said. "Eventually I'll attempt to travel to my home, but until I have completely recuperated from my dreadful experience in Lawrence, I'll take accommodations at a Mrs. Naomi Kling's boardinghouse."

Ma put down the stirring spoon she was holding. "I know Mrs. Kling. She's a respectable widow, and I have nothing but good to say about her boardinghouse. I've even heard that, in spite of shortages, she sets the best table in St. Joseph. But her lodgings are expensive."

Smiling at Ma, Miss Hennessey said, "I've imposed upon your kind hospitality long enough, Noreen. You, John, and Peg have been a second family to me. I can't thank you enough for your many kindnesses."

"We've been glad to help," Ma answered.

"You did help me—even more than you know. I realize now, after these days of peaceful shelter in your home, that my early fears were irrational. I'm no longer afraid."

"Good." Ma smiled broadly and wiped her hands on her apron. "Just remember that at any time in the future, if you need our help, you have only to ask and it will be given."

"Thank you," Miss Hennessey said demurely. A hand crept out from under her shawl, and she gave Peg an envelope. "Peg, dear, I understand there is a stable on Penn Street. Will you please be so kind as to deliver this to the stable owner for me? My letter gives the necessary instructions. A driver will be sent to take me to Mrs. Kling's."

"So soon?" Ma asked.

"I've imposed enough," Miss Hennessey said. She hugged Ma and Peg, murmuring, "Hurry, now," to Peg and dashed back upstairs.

"She's been welcome here, Ma," Peg said in bewilderment. "She said we were like family. So why does she want to stay with a stranger?"

"It's her decision, not ours, love," Ma answered.

But Peg was puzzled. Into her mind popped the face of Miss Hennessey's cousin. But he was leaving . . . for a place far away, Miss Hennessey had said. Surely her decision to leave the Murphy home had nothing to do with him.

5

PEG RAN DOWN the hill and over a few blocks to Penn Street, which was one of the busiest streets in St. Joseph. In spite of the war and the occasional abandoned and boarded-up stores, the street was crowded with horse-drawn buggies and wagons and carts pulled by oxen. There were horseback riders aplenty, winding their way past men dressed in buckskin and women carrying market baskets. The air was filled with the pungent smell of horse droppings and sweat-stained leather. Peg wrinkled her nose and wove through the conglomeration, dodging and ducking, until she reached the stables and handed Miss Hennessey's letter to the man in charge.

"Tell the lady I'll be by for her at four o'clock," he said.

Peg's mission accomplished, she stopped as she

reached the hotel, remembering again her visit here with the Swensons and Danny. Oh, how she missed her brother Danny!

Because they'd been close in age, Peg had always had a special love for Danny. It had been terribly hard when she'd gone to live with Ma, and Danny had chosen to stay with Alfrid Swenson.

"Alfrid's gentle and kind, like Da was," Danny had attempted to explain. "He's my father now, Peg, and I love him. I need him, and he needs me, too. I can't leave him. Do you understand?"

Peg tried to understand, but there were many times when she missed Danny so much she could hardly bear the loneliness. Although Danny periodically came to town with Alfrid Swenson and Ennie, the woman Alfrid had married after Olga died, his time with Ma and Peg was always brief. Remembering how she'd clung to Danny in this hotel, yet how she'd insisted he not be allowed to eat more than his share of the cookies that were served, tears rushed to Peg's eyes.

Soon after the onset of the war the hotel had been turned into Union Army headquarters. Here were the offices of Colonel John Williams, commander of the St. Joseph Military District; and General John Bassett, the provost marshal, whose job it was to find and arrest spies and Rebs. Uncomfortably, Peg thought about Miss Hennessey's cousin James. In a way, like it or not, Peg had helped him to escape. Luckily the provost marshal would never find out about it. Peg would hate to be sent to prison.

Eager to take another look at the elegant lobby with its beautiful red Brussels carpets and carved, winding staircase, Peg clattered across the wooden sidewalk and held out a hand to grasp the handle of the heavy door.

"Stop!" a voice ordered.

Peg froze, her hand dropping to her side. She looked up at the Union soldier who had appeared out of nowhere to block the door.

"You have no business here, little girl," he said. "Get along home."

"I just wanted to see the lobby of the hotel," Peg told him. "It used to be beautiful."

"I don't know what it used to look like," the soldier answered, "but it sure ain't beautiful anymore."

Peg didn't answer. Tears blurring her vision, she turned and fled.

When the buggy arrived Peg was caught in a whirl of profuse thanks and hugs. Miss Hennessey leaned forward to give one last wave, then was gone.

"She didn't say she'd see us again," Peg complained. "She didn't ask us to come to Mrs. Kling's boardinghouse to visit her." A hurt tear slid down her nose, and she angrily brushed it away.

Ma put an arm around Peg's shoulders and steered her to the parlor sofa. As they sat close together Ma said, "Miss Hennessey needed us for only a short time, love. She doesn't need us now."

"It's not a matter of needing us. I thought she was my—our friend."

"Only a few friendships last forever. You'll find, as you grow older, that most friendships come and go."

Peg squirmed away from her mother's arm. "There you go again, Ma, talking as if I'm a child."

"You'll have to admit that you don't know all there is to know at the age of eleven." Ma gave Peg a teasing smile, and, in spite of her irritation, Peg couldn't keep from smiling back.

As she settled against her mother's arm, Peg

thought about Miss Hennessey, who at first had been nervous and frail and frightened of her own shadow. During the week, as Miss Hennessey's health improved, she had seemed at times, in quick unguarded moments, to be as self-assured as Ma or Miss Thomas, which was totally at odds with her usual quiet, timid nature. Peg remembered that instant on the stairs in which Miss Hennessey had appeared to be a vibrant, handsome woman, and she thought of the resonant beauty of her voice as she read aloud *A Tale of Two Cities.* Surely, Peg wondered, she hadn't imagined all that. Or had she?

Well, it scarcely mattered now. Miss Hennessey had left, and Peg had lost a friend. "I'll bring down the towels and the sheets from her bed," Peg said and climbed to her feet.

"You're a good, dear girl," Ma told her.

Peg didn't feel like a good, dear girl. She felt like kicking the table leg, or raising a ruckus, or chasing Marcus all the way home, the way she had when he'd called her a skinny ninny.

It wasn't until she'd scooped up an armful of linens that a glint of metal caught her eye and she noticed one of Miss Hennessey's shawls that had fallen behind the chair in the corner. A small, circular, silver pin was still attached.

Peg folded and smoothed the shawl, laid it on top of the linens, and took it downstairs to give to Ma.

"It's getting late, so I'll send it to her tomorrow," Ma said, then paused and smiled at Peg. "Better yet, when you come home from school, could you take it to her?"

"Oh, yes!" Peg answered quickly. She'd love an excuse to see Miss Hennessey again. Maybe by tomorrow afternoon Miss Hennessey would have realized that

Mrs. Kling's boardinghouse wasn't as comfortable and homey as the Murphys' house, and she'd come back and stay with them until she was ready to travel home.

As Peg went about her studies and evening chores she could think of little else than seeing Miss Hennessey again. The next day she wiggled and fidgeted so much in class that Miss Thomas said, "Peg Kelly, I declare! You've been squirming as though there's a bug down your back. Now settle down and pay attention."

Marcus, who sat behind Peg, leaned forward and whispered, "There *is* a bug down your back. It's a black beetle with six wiggly legs and sharp pointed teeth. And if it can find any meat on your bones, it will bite!"

He gave her neck a sharp pinch, and Peg shuddered. It did feel like a bug! But she clamped her teeth together and ignored him. It was hard to ignore the odor coming from Marcus, however. Every time his mother wondered if she'd seen a nit in his hair she doused his head in kerosene oil; and, even though it was only the beginning of October, she'd already hung a small bag of garlic around his neck to ward off the fall catarrh and had sewn him into his long underwear for the winter.

He pulled his treasured obsidian arrowhead from his pocket and dangled it next to her. It was tempting to try to snatch it, knowing that such a long, finely tapered obsidian arrowhead was rare in these parts, but Peg didn't move.

Marcus, who didn't like being ignored, kicked the back of Peg's bench. She refused to respond, gleefully knowing this would bother him more than anything else she could do. Marcus was such a . . . a child!

After school Peg ran all the way home. She brushed and brushed her hair, unable to tame her wild red curls, so she tied a sunbonnet over her hair, picked up the shawl and silver pin, and set out to visit Miss Hennessey.

Hugging the shawl close to protect it as she hurried through the crowds, Peg followed Ma's instructions and rang the bell of Mrs. Kling's boardinghouse.

"I'm Peg Kelly, and I've come to see Miss Violet Hennessey, please," she told the round, rosy woman who opened the door.

The woman tucked a loose strand of gray-streaked hair into the bun that rested like a fat biscuit on top of her head. "Peg Kelly? Kelly? And who might your people be?" she asked.

"My mother is Noreen Kel—Murphy," Peg answered. "She's married to John Murphy, the blacksmith."

Smiling broadly, the woman said, "Of course, of course. I'm Mrs. Kling, child. Come inside, please."

As soon as the door had shut behind her, Peg glanced around the large, ornate parlor. The windows were decorated with lace curtains, dark velvet swags dipping across the tops. There were crocheted, white doilies of every size on all the tables and on the backs and arms of the overstuffed chairs. Paintings of landscapes and of flowers covered the walls, and oil lamps with hand-painted flowers on their glass chimneys were placed throughout the room.

"Miss Hennessey isn't here at the moment," Mrs. Kling told Peg.

"Oh," Peg said. Disappointed, she slumped against a high-backed wing chair, resting her chin on the shawl and trying to think of what to do next. She could leave the shawl with Mrs. Kling to deliver to Miss Hennessey, but that would rob her of the visit she'd planned.

She straightened, taking a deep breath. "Is it all right if I wait for her to return?"

"Of course," Mrs. Kling said. "Just find yourself a comfy seat. I don't think you'll have to wait long."

As Mrs. Kling left the room, Peg sat in the wing chair, but soon two boarders, wearing black frock coats and trousers and stovepipe hats, entered and stared with curiosity at Peg as they made their way to the staircase. Not wanting to be on exhibit, Peg moved to a chair back against the farthest wall under the leaves of a large potted plant.

Peg had waited scarcely half an hour when the door opened, and a beautiful woman entered, her right hand resting lightly on her escort's arm. She was dressed in a full skirt and short, fitted jacket in a pale blue wool. A tiny, feathered hat perched on top of her dark curls. The man spoke, and as the woman looked up at him, laughing in delight at whatever he had said, he beamed in pleasure.

Peg caught her breath in astonishment. Miss Hennessey! The beautiful woman was Miss Violet Hennessey! And she was with the terrible, horrible Mr. Amos Crandon!

Too stunned to move or speak, Peg could only watch as Miss Hennessey said, "Thank you, Mr. Crandon, for your very kind help. Without your assistance I might never have been able to see General Bassett."

"It was my great pleasure to assist you, Miss Hennessey," Mr. Crandon said. His cheeks puffed with pleasure, making him look like an ugly, giant frog in Peg's opinion. "As soon as General Bassett's letter guaranteeing you safe passage has been written and signed, I'll personally deliver it to you. Perhaps tonight. At the latest, tomorrow."

"I shall be forever grateful to you, Mr. Crandon," Miss Hennessey said.

Beaming even more broadly, Mr. Crandon bowed low over Miss Hennessey's hand, then opened the door and left.

This woman who simpered over the despicable Mr. Crandon was not the Miss Hennessey Peg knew as a friend. Something strange was taking place—something she didn't understand.

I'll face right up to Miss Hennessey, Peg told herself, *and find out once and for all exactly who she is and what's going on!*

6

<hr>

"Miss Hennessey!" Peg called out and jumped to her feet.

As Miss Hennessey whirled toward Peg, the remnants of her smile vanished, and she looked as though she were frantically trying to recall what Peg may have overheard. "Peg! It's you," she said.

"Yes, ma'am, it's me," Peg answered. She held out the shawl. "You left this shawl and pin at our house. I thought you'd need it." She paused, staring at the beautiful blue outfit. "But I guess you don't."

Miss Hennessey reached out—not for the shawl, but for Peg—and drew her close. Warm and friendly again she said, "Peg, dear, what a lovely surprise! It's wonderful to see you. I've missed our delightful conversations. How nice of you to come to see me."

Peg allowed herself to be led to a nearby sofa,

where Miss Hennessey pulled her down beside her, but she didn't smile in return. "You were with Mr. Crandon," she said.

Miss Hennessey's eyes twinkled. "Why, yes. A charming, very helpful man. Do you know him?"

"Mr. Crandon's *not* charming or helpful! He's a mean, nasty old humbug who tries to hornswoggle everybody he can!"

Embarrassed when she saw that she had shocked Miss Hennessey by her outburst, Peg stared down at her toes. "I'm sorry I used unladylike language, ma'am, but it's true."

"I was under the impression that Mr. Crandon is a highly respected businessman in St. Joseph."

"He's richer than most folks. Maybe some people think that's a reason to respect him, but I don't. First he was a southern sympathizer. Now he's for the Union. 'All he's interested in is whatever side his bread is buttered on,' Ma says. He's been rude and hateful to Ma and to Mike . . . to all of us Kellys."

"Then I don't like him, either." Miss Hennessey smiled and squeezed Peg's hand. "In the future I'll have as little as possible to do with him."

"He said he was coming back with a letter," Peg reminded.

Miss Hennessey nodded, the long feather on her hat brushing Peg's forehead. "I've recently received word that my sister and her husband are temporarily residing south of St. Joseph in Buchanan County!"

"Your sister?"

"Yes! My sister, Nellie Parker."

"But I thought you said you lost your family in Boston."

"My parents. Not my sister." Producing a handkerchief from a pocket in the sleeve of her jacket, Miss

Hennessey held it to her lips and closed her eyes tightly.

Miserable at the anguish she had caused Miss Hennessey, Peg stammered, "I'm sorry. I didn't mean to—"

"Of course you didn't. It's quite all right." Miss Hennessey opened her eyes and clasped her hands together under her chin. "Oh, Peg, you can't imagine how much I long to see my sister! But with Union patrols throughout the countryside—many of them treating loyal members of the Union as rebels, simply because they live in Missouri—I wouldn't dare to travel even a short distance without an official letter guaranteeing me safe passage. That's the letter to which Mr. Crandon referred."

Peg frowned and held up two fingers pressed together. "Everybody knows that Mr. Crandon and the provost marshal are as thick as that."

"That's why he's able to obtain the letter for me."

A sudden thought struck Peg, and she blurted out, "You haven't been in St. Joseph long. How did you know to ask Mr. Crandon for help?"

Miss Hennessey smiled. "I met him when I opened a small account at his bank. As we chatted I made bold to tell him my wish to visit my sister and, to my delight, he informed me of his strong political connections and offered his help."

The explanation made perfect sense, yet Peg still felt vaguely uncomfortable. She took a deep breath and spoke in a rush. "You're so different. You don't even look like yourself."

"I'm not surprised." Miss Hennessey stood up and turned from side to side. "Do you like my dress? I'm so partial to blue. Blue is your color, too, Peg, with that glorious red curly hair."

"Your dress is very pretty," Peg said, "but it's not like the dresses you wore when you stayed with us."

"Of course not," Miss Hennessey said. "A dress like this would not be at all suitable for wear in the home. You have party dresses that you save for special occasions, do you not?"

"I have a dress with a pleated skirt and a lace-trimmed collar that I wear to church," Peg admitted.

"There. You see?"

"I suppose so." Peg knew that Ma would have a conniption fit if she wore her good dress around the house. Peg tried to brush away her niggling suspicions, but found it getting harder and harder to do. There were so many strange and puzzling things about Miss Hennessey. And yet Miss Hennessey always seemed to offer logical answers.

"I'm starving," Miss Hennessey said. "I'm going to ask Mrs. Kling if we might have a cup of tea and perhaps a sweet to enjoy with it. Would you like that?"

Peg didn't have to be asked twice. She waited patiently while Miss Hennessey entered the hallway in search of Mrs. Kling.

"May my guest and I please have some tea and shortbread, if you have some?" Peg heard Miss Hennessey ask.

She also heard Mrs. Kling say, "No trouble at all, Miss Hennessey. Here . . . I was just looking for you. A fine-looking young man left this letter for you about an hour ago. He asked me to give it to you the moment you came in. Urgent, he said, and he couldn't wait."

A fine-looking young man? Could he have been James? Peg doubted that Miss Hennessey had been in St. Joe long enough to meet other fine-looking young men. She wished she could ask Miss Hennessey if James were in St. Joe and if he might finally be paying heed to her pleas to give his loyalty to the Union, instead of to Quantrill. But she couldn't. As Ma sometimes said, "There's a big step between natural curiosity and prying."

When Miss Hennessey finally returned, Peg searched her face, but she saw neither sorrow nor joy. Instead, her eyes seemed overbright, and her hands trembled as she placed a tray with cups, saucers, a pot of tea, and a plate of shortbread cookies on a low table.

One look at the tea and cookies caused painful memories that drove all other thoughts from Peg's mind, and her heart ached. "On the day my brothers and sisters and I arrived in St. Joe, I had tea poured from a fancy pot just like that," she said. "Mr. and Mrs. Swenson chose Danny and me to live with them, and before we rode to the Swensons' farm, Mrs. Swenson insisted that we stop at the hotel for tea."

Miss Hennessey poured two steaming cups of fragrant tea and placed one in front of Peg. "You must miss your brothers and sisters very much," she said.

Peg nodded. "I do. All of them. But especially Danny. Because he's just little more than two years older than me, we were always special chums."

"I heard about Frances daring to work with the Underground Railroad and about Mike's bravery in serving as a drummer boy with our Union Army." Miss Hennessey paused a moment, then said, "I've known you long enough, Peg, to be sure that you're every bit as resourceful and brave as your brother and sister. If you were faced with a challenge, as they were, you'd meet it without question."

Taken by surprise, Peg murmured, "I—I suppose. I—I don't know."

"Well, I do." Miss Hennessey smiled and held the

cookie plate out to Peg. "Do have a cookie. They're delicious." She studied Peg so intently that Peg knew it wasn't cookies Miss Hennessey had in mind. What was she thinking?

Peg bit into the buttery, crumbly shortbread, still warm from the oven.

"It's such an amazing coincidence that your brother Danny lives near my sister. As I've just told you, I've been yearning to pay my sister a visit, but under the current circumstances I've hesitated to travel alone." She tilted her head and smiled at Peg. "However, I wonder if . . ."

Peg's heart pounded as she realized that Miss Hennessey might be considering her and Ma as traveling companions. She held her breath, waiting for the invitation, and was disappointed when it didn't come.

Miss Hennessey pulled a tiny watch from the pocket of her jacket. "Dear me," she said. "It's getting late, and your mother will be worried. Please, Peg dear, explain that your delay was all my fault, and ask her . . . No." Her eyes twinkled as if she knew a wonderful secret. "I'll see her soon and ask her myself."

As Peg walked home she thought about Miss Hennessey's secret. With all her heart she hoped it had to do with traveling with her to see her sister. And Danny!

It must! She gave a skip and a jump as she thought of seeing Danny again. And soon! Ma'd be excited to go, too.

I wish . . . I wish . . . Afraid to put her wish into actual words, for fear it wouldn't come true, Peg began to hum "Camptown Races," concentrating as hard as she could.

"Skinny ninny!"

A stone skittered across the road in front of her

feet, and Marcus's head popped up on the other side of a nearby holly hedge.

"Marcus! You . . . you . . . guttersnipe!" Peg shouted.

She chased him until he slammed into the door of his house. His mother began yelling at him for making so much racket, and Peg grinned in satisfaction. Her own house was just a short way up the road, so she kept running, bounded into the kitchen, and flopped into a chair.

"Good gracious!" Ma said as she pumped a glass of water at the sink and handed it to Peg, who was breathing heavily. "What happened to you?"

Peg gulped noisily and put down the glass. "Marcus called me a skinny ninny again, and I chased him. Lucky for stupid old Marcus I didn't catch him."

Ma chuckled. "This was *after* you returned Miss Hennessey's shawl, I hope."

Peg nodded.

"Did you find Miss Hennessey well?"

"Yes." Peg hesitated, wondering about all she'd seen and heard. How could she describe it to Ma?

"You were gone for quite a while. Did you have a nice visit?"

"We had tea. Tea and shortbread."

"That's lovely," Ma said. When Peg didn't continue, Ma asked, "Will you set the table for me, please? John will be home soon."

Peg slowly got to her feet, ambled to the cupboard and removed three plates. "Ma," she said, "Miss Hennessey was . . . well, different."

"How was she different?"

"Her hair was curled and piled on her head, and she was wearing a blue dress and jacket and a hat with feathers."

"That's nice," Ma said. "It shows she's feeling well enough to take a few pains with her appearance."

"That's the reason? That's all?" Peg asked. She felt such a surge of relief at Ma's explanation that she quickly slapped the plates on the table and reached for the napkins.

Ma looked at her sharply. "Is something bothering you, Peg?"

"Not really. Well . . . I don't know. Could I ask you something, Ma?"

"Of course," Ma answered.

Peg placed forks and knives at each plate, then plopped down onto the hard wooden chair. "Miss Hennessey was out when I got to Mrs. Kling's boardinghouse, so I waited for her. When she came in she was with Mr. Crandon." Peg made a face. "He kissed her hand. Ugh! Frog lips!"

Ma's eyes widened in surprise. "She was with Mr. Crandon? Are you sure?"

"Yes, I'm sure. I *saw* him, Ma. So when Miss Hennessey and I were talking I told her what a hornswoggling . . ."

"Watch your language, miss," Ma warned.

"I told her why I didn't like him. She said then she didn't like him either, but she's going to see him again because he's getting a letter for her."

"What kind of letter?" Ma sat across from Peg, leaning toward her.

Delighted to have Ma's full attention, Peg explained about Miss Hennessey's sister and the letter of safe passage she needed to get from the provost marshal.

When Peg had finished Ma leaned back and nodded. "So Violet has a sister nearby. My, my. All this time I mistakenly thought she had no family left. Well, of course she'd want to see her sister."

She reached out and brushed the tangled curly fringe from Peg's forehead. "Sometimes, love, we have to deal with officials who are so self-important they are not interested in helping people who ask them for help. I've heard of a few others' unfortunate attempts to see the provost marshal—like John's friend, Julian Cassidy, who was wrongly suspected of being a southern sympathizer and his barn burned to the ground. It makes me doubt that Miss Hennessey could get past all the officials in the military district headquarters standing between her and the provost marshal without some help."

"Even if it's Mr. Crandon who's helping her?"

"Even if it's Mr. Crandon."

It was comforting talking to Ma, Peg decided. Ma had the answers to all the questions that had been bothering her. "Ma," she said, "Miss Hennessey's going to come to see you."

"That's nice," Ma said. "Did she say when?"

"No. Just that she's coming." Peg nearly bit her tongue trying to keep from saying any more about the visit. If she said aloud her wish to see Danny, then it might not come true. After all, it was nothing but a wish. Miss Hennessey hadn't said one word about Ma and Peg going with her. That had been Peg's idea.

At that moment John Murphy clomped into the house with a bear hug for Ma and a big smile for Peg, and the conversation changed to the latest news about the war.

"It's not the best of news," John told them. "Our Federal boys lost a major battle to the Rebs in Chickamauga, Georgia. I heard there were over thirty-four thousand dead, counting both sides."

Ma shuddered and made the Sign of the Cross.

Peg tried to imagine how many people would make

up thirty-four thousand, but it was such an enormous amount that she couldn't.

"So Major General William Rosecrans retreated, taking what was left of his army into Chattanooga," Mr. Murphy said. "The Rebs have the city and our army under siege by cutting off any supplies that might come by way of the river."

"When will all this horror end?" Ma murmured.

"When we beat the Rebs, Noreen my girl. It's as simple as that."

"Soon, I hope and pray."

"I'm afraid it's going to get worse before it gets better."

Ma's voice quavered. "So many wounded, so many dead."

"Miss Thomas's brother came back from fighting the war because he was wounded," Peg said. "He lost an eye and wears a big black patch over the hole where his eye used to be."

Ma thumped a chair against the table. "Stop! That's enough of this talk! I can't bear it! It could have been Mike who was injured or killed!"

Peg's memory of Mike was strong. When he passed through St. Joe after his days as a drummer in the Union Army, he'd been sunburned, thinner, and more muscular than before, and his eyes had been dark with horrors he'd never forget.

"Tell me about the battles. Tell me what happened to you," Peg had asked, eager to know what Mike had been through, the better to share his problems.

But Mike's eyes had closed, and he'd turned away. "You wouldn't want to know," he'd replied so firmly that Peg hadn't dared to ask again; but after she'd gone to bed she'd heard, from down the stairway, the sound of voices and Ma's occasional murmuring and weeping.

Ma closed her eyes, took a deep breath, then opened her eyes again. Calmly she said, "Supper's ready, and it's time for both of you to wash up."

Later, after supper, the warm fragrance of the kitchen, Ma's soft humming over her mending, and John's deep, rumbling voice now and then reading aloud an interesting bit from his newspaper, wove a cocoon of contentment that shut out all thoughts of war from Peg's mind.

Sleepily, Peg remembered that the next day would be Saturday. She'd help Ma with the laundry and the ironing to follow, and she wouldn't have to go to school. May would probably come to visit when her family chores were over. Maybe they could make cornhusk dolls for May's little sister. Or lie in wait for Marcus and Willie and throw weed clumps at them. It might be fun to plot how to get Marcus's lucky arrowhead away from him. It was the most precious thing he owned, and he always carried it with him.

Peg jumped when she heard a loud knock at the front door.

"Who in the world could that be?" Ma asked.

John strode to open the door, Ma and Peg right behind him.

A boy tipped his hat and handed John an envelope.

John fished in his pocket for a coin and gave it to the boy. As he shut the door he said, "It's a letter for you, Noreen. It has your name on it."

Ma tore open the envelope and pulled out a creamy sheet of paper. "For goodness sakes," she said. "It's a note from Miss Hennessey. She's coming to see us bright and early tomorrow morning."

"A strange time to come calling," Mr. Murphy said.

"Especially when she's aware that Saturday's the day I do the washing." Ma shrugged. "Why did she have to pick Saturday morning?"

Peg knew why. She had to be right! She clasped her hands together tightly, hoping with all her strength that her wish was going to come true, that Miss Hennessey was going to ask Ma and Peg to come with her to visit her sister—and Danny! Ma would agree.

Or would she?

Peg was tempted to beg and plead with Ma right now, just to make sure, but she couldn't. Miss Hennessey hadn't even asked yet.

7

ALL DURING THE night Peg's sleep was fitful. She crept downstairs the next morning while it was still dark, lit the oil lamps, and started a fire in the stove. By the time Ma came down to begin cooking breakfast, Peg had set the table, filled the tea kettle, and melted a little pork fat in a skillet, ready to fry flapjacks.

"I made the batter," Peg said proudly.

Ma measured tea into a pot and poured in the boiling water. "You're my morning sleepyhead. What pulled you out of bed so early?" She put the pot in the center of the table, paused as though she'd suddenly remembered something, and smiled teasingly. "Does your early rising have anything to do with Miss Hennessey's visit?"

"I couldn't sleep, Ma," Peg mumbled. She gave an

extra stir to the batter and dropped spoonfuls into the sizzling pan.

"She surely won't be coming this early."

"I know."

Ma put a hand on Peg's shoulder and turned her so that Peg was looking into her eyes. "And what else do you know, love?"

"Nothing real, Ma. Just guesses," Peg answered honestly.

Ma picked up a broad spatula and reached across Peg to flip over the flapjacks. "You said Miss Hennessey's sister lives nearby. Exactly where is *nearby?*"

With effort Peg kept herself from groaning aloud. Could Ma read minds? Unable to meet Ma's gaze, Peg shrugged and said, "When Miss Hennessey gets here you can ask her."

Ma set a heaping plate of flapjacks on the table. "Sit down and eat, love." She nodded toward the stairs, which creaked under John's heavy footsteps. "I'll make the next batch for John."

John didn't like to talk before breakfast, and Ma said nothing more about Miss Hennessey, to Peg's relief.

After John had left for his blacksmith's shop Ma pinned up her sleeves and laid a fire on the cement block in the back yard. She placed the large, heavy boiler pan on a support over the fire, and she and Peg carried buckets of water to half-fill the boiler. Ma poured lumps of soft lye soap into the water and stirred the mixture with a long, thick stick until the soap had melted. Peg helped carry out armsful of soiled clothing, sheets, and towels, some of which were dropped into the simmering water, which Ma stirred endlessly, back and forth.

Peg, on the other hand, listened for the sound of

horses' hooves and buggy's wheels. Where was Miss Hennessey? It was already close to eight o'clock. Why hadn't she come?

Peg jumped as a voice spoke from the open kitchen door. "Noreen! Peg! No one answered my knock, so I just walked in."

Ma put down the stirring stick and smiled, as she wiped her hands on her apron. "You're always welcome in our house, Violet. You know that."

Miss Hennessey sailed down the steps of the back porch stoop in a trim brown traveling costume.

"My, aren't you looking grand!" Ma said. "Would you like a cup of tea? We can leave the wash for a while."

As she glanced at the boiler and the pile of clothing on the ground, Miss Hennessey frowned. "Oh, dear! In my excitement, I didn't stop to think."

"Excitement?" Ma asked.

"My sister Nellie! Did Peg tell you? I heard from Nellie, and discovered that she and my brother-in-law, Louis Parker, are now living on a farm right here in Buchanan County, south of St. Joseph!"

"That's lovely for you," Ma said. "You said *south* of St. Joseph?"

"Yes! Very near to the Swensons' farm where your son Danny lives." Miss Hennessey ducked her head, almost as shy and apologetic as she had been when she first came to St. Joseph. "In my foolishness I rented a horse and buggy. I was so sure that you and Peg would ride with me. It would give you the opportunity to visit with Danny."

Ma held out an arm toward the washing. "As you see, I can't get away, Violet. Not today."

Miss Hennessey took Ma's hand and squeezed it between her own. "Of course," she said apologetically.

"I was so thoughtless not to have invited you ahead of time."

Embarrassed, Ma began, "Violet, you were not thoughtless."

But Miss Hennessey interrupted, her eyes dark with misery as she pleaded, "Oh, Noreen, will you please allow Peg to come with me, even though you can't?"

Peg gasped as she heard Miss Hennessey add, "Maybe some women are brave enough to travel alone, but I'm not. Peg and I will be good company for each other, and I assure you she'll be perfectly safe. I even have a letter of safe passage signed by the provost marshal himself, in case we meet up with any patrols."

"Patrols," Ma repeated and frowned.

"We have no reason to fear the patrols." Miss Hennessey's eyes met Peg's as she said, "Peg is not afraid."

Whatever qualms Peg felt about leaving Ma and traveling alone with Miss Hennessey vanished immediately. "Ma!" she cried, "The patrols are Union! They're on *our* side!"

Miss Hennessey took a deep breath and spoke rapidly, not giving Ma a chance to object. "It's the southern counties that have had so much conflict between patrols and bushwhackers. During the last few months there has been little trouble in Buchanan County. We'll be safe. I promise! I assure you I wouldn't make the trip myself if I thought otherwise."

Twice Ma had opened her mouth to speak, but was unable to break into Miss Hennessey's plea. Now, however, she spoke up firmly. "My mind wouldn't be easy if Peg were away from home."

"Ma!" Peg wailed. "I'm not afraid of patrols! The army's there to protect us! And if I go with Miss Hennessey, I could visit Danny!"

To Peg's surprise Miss Hennessey let go of Ma's hand, pulled a handkerchief from her reticule, and dabbed at her eyes. "You're right, Noreen," she said. "You're right to feel that even though Peg would be under my constant, loving protection, I could never be able to take care of her as well as you could."

Ma's face turned pink and she fumbled for words. "That's not what I meant, Violet."

"I was so foolish to hope," Violet murmured into her handkerchief. "I haven't seen my sister for at least five years, and all I've been able to think of has been Nellie with her dear smile and happy ways. I should have asked you first. I shouldn't have depleted my much needed funds to rent the horse and buggy." She gave a loud sniffle.

"Oh, dear. Come inside and sit down," Ma murmured. "We'll have that cup of tea while you tell me about your sister."

A rush of excitement warmed Peg's chest. Was Ma weakening?

Peg filled the kettle and listened quietly as Miss Hennessey said, "Nellie is two years younger than I am. She married just before our parents died—a good match with a fine man. Louis Parker is one of the Virginia Parkers."

"I thought you said your family lived in Boston."

"They did, but very briefly. My grandmother on my father's side was becoming frail, so my parents moved to Boston to care for her. Then one day on the street . . . a runaway horse . . ." Miss Hennessey broke down and sobbed into her handkerchief.

Ma got up and brought her a dry one. She patted Miss Hennessey's shoulder and said, "I'm so sorry that I brought up unhappy memories."

Miss Hennessey wiped her eyes. "It's all right,

Noreen. I just hope you can understand how alone I felt, with Nellie and Louis so far away. You can imagine how thrilled I was when I discovered they're now close at hand."

"Perhaps they can visit you in St. Joseph," Ma said.

Violet climbed to her feet, her shoulders drooping. "Perhaps," she murmured, but there was no hope in her voice.

Ma stood, too. She took a long look at Peg, then turned back to Violet. "You'll have Peg home again before too late?"

"Before dark. I promise."

Peg sucked in her breath. "Please, Ma?" she whispered.

"If it weren't for the possibilities that patrols might stop you . . ."

Miss Hennessey pulled a folded piece of paper from her reticule and gave it to Ma. "Here's the letter General John Bassett wrote for me. You can see it's official. No one will stop us. Besides, there has been very little action lately in Buchanan County."

"That's true," Ma admitted slowly, "but—"

"Please!" Peg begged.

With a sigh Ma gave in. "All right," she said. "Peg, put on your dress with the pleated skirt and for goodness sakes find a pair of stockings without a hole in them, and take a shawl. It's warm now, but the weather may change, and brush your hair and . . ."

Peg, her heart jumping with excitement, had never dressed so fast. She felt grown-up and brave and independent, and the best part was that she would soon see Danny again!

She accepted the sunbonnet Ma gave her and tied the bow to one side, rather than under her chin, all the while pretending it was an elegant, feathered hat.

She had time for a quick hug for Ma before she climbed into the buggy and set off with Miss Hennessey on their journey.

As they rode through town, Miss Hennessey chatted pleasantly about Miss Kling's excellent food and told Peg amusing stories about some of the other boarders.

"How long will you stay in St. Joseph?" Peg asked.

"That depends upon circumstances," Miss Hennessey answered. "Mostly financial."

Peg wasn't sure how much it cost to stay at a boardinghouse, but Ma had mentioned the word *expensive* when she'd talked about Mrs. Kling's boardinghouse to Mr. Murphy. "Why don't you stay with your sister and her husband?" she suggested.

Miss Hennessey gave a flick to the reins, guiding the horse across the ruts in the road, before she looked down at Peg and smiled. "Their visit in this area is only temporary," she said.

But so is yours, Peg thought. *Oh, well.* She put the problem out of her mind. Grown-ups had their own way of thinking about things, and sometimes made them more complicated than they needed to be. Like when Ma had agreed to come to Missouri and marry Alfrid Swenson but instead fell in love with John Murphy, which left Mr. Swenson without a wife, so he married Ennie Pratka. Then Danny chose to stay with the Swensons, and Peg chose to live with Ma. *Oh, Danny, Danny, Danny!* Peg thought. *Won't you be surprised to see me!*

The horse moved at a quick trot, and very soon they left St. Joseph behind. As the road followed the low, rolling hillside, Peg sucked in a deep breath of the warm air, lush with the damply bitter fragrance of tall grass.

"It's so peaceful here," she said. "I love the countryside."

"I do, too." Miss Hennessey smiled. "Away from the noise of constantly creaking cartwheels and the clop of horses and . . ."

Peg, startled as Miss Hennessey broke off, followed her gaze to a bend in the road ahead. Six Union soldiers, their uniforms streaked with dust, rode toward them.

As the soldiers approached, a sergeant at the front of the group held up a hand, and Miss Hennessey quickly pulled her horse to a stop.

Peg held her breath, frightened in spite of the fact that these were Union soldiers, here to uphold the law under martial rule. She and Miss Hennessey had done nothing wrong.

Three of the soldiers were young and seemed uninterested in either the buggy or its passengers, but one man, whose beard was shaggy and dirty with crumbs from recent meals, searched the wagon with his eyes, his gaze coming to rest on Miss Hennessey's reticule, which lay on the buggy seat.

Miss Hennessey's gloved hands gripped the reins tightly, but her voice gave no indication of her nervousness. Instead, she smiled sweetly and said, "Good morning, Captain."

"Not *captain*, ma'am. It's just *sergeant*," he gruffed, but his chest swelled with self-importance. "Where are you bound for?"

"My daughter and I are going to visit my sister," Miss Hennessey told him.

Daughter? Peg was startled. *Why did Miss Hennessey lie?*

Miss Hennessey fumbled through her reticule and pulled out the letter promising safe passage. "General

---

John Bassett, the provost marshal of St. Joseph, gave this to me."

The sergeant dutifully examined the letter, then handed it back. "You live in St. Joseph?"

"Yes."

"Where does your sister live?"

"In Buchanan County. On River Road."

He quickly glanced inside the buggy. "You haven't got traveling bags with you, so I take it you don't plan to stay long."

"That's right. Just today."

"I'd caution you not to return after dark. There's no telling who you might run into on these back roads."

From the corner of her eye Peg shot a quick glance at the soldier with the beard, who was still looking at the reticule. *Union Army or not, I'd hate to run into this one anywhere!* Peg thought.

"You may proceed," the sergeant said.

Miss Hennessey smiled again, picked up the reins, and clucked to the horse. The soldiers rode past them with a great clatter, stirring up clouds of dust that caused Peg to cough.

The moment they were out of hearing Peg asked, "Why did you say I was your daughter?"

"Not now." Miss Hennessey's voice was low and quick.

"What do you mean, not now? I—"

"Hush!"

To Peg's amazement Miss Hennessey pulled a small handgun from her reticule and tucked it on the seat under her skirt. In a low voice she said, "Whatever may happen next, don't be afraid."

8

Peg stiffened as the beat of horse hooves rapidly approached their buggy. A voice shouted, "Pull up! Be quick about it!"

The bearded soldier appeared, rising above the kicked-up eddies of road dust like an evil spirit. He jerked his horse to a stop and leaned into the buggy, reaching with a large, grubby hand for Miss Hennessey's reticule. "Give me that bag," he ordered.

Peg flinched as she was hit with the sour, stinking odor that poured from his breath and his body, but Miss Hennessey calmly said, "You'll not take my letter."

"I don't want your letter," he snapped. "I want money."

Miss Hennessey paused for only a moment, then obediently handed him her reticule. She held the reins with her left hand and quietly slid her right hand to the buggy seat, where it rested against her handgun.

Peg was too frightened to move as she stared at the large revolver in the soldier's belt. Surely, Miss Hennessey's small pistol would be no match for that!

Barely able to get his large hand inside the drawstring opening, the soldier fished around, then triumphantly withdrew it. A quick flash of paper bills disappeared into his fist as he handed back the reticule.

"Where's your jewelry?" he asked.

Miss Hennessey met his gaze. "I have none with me," she said. "I wouldn't be foolish enough to wear it."

The soldier jerked again on his horse's reins, wheeling him around, and galloped back down the road.

Peg leaned from the buggy and peered after him. "He stole your money!" she cried.

"Only two dollars."

With peppermints selling at five for a penny, two dollars seemed like a lot of money to Peg. "You aren't angry?"

Miss Hennessey shook her head. "I was prepared for theft."

Confused and hurt, Peg demanded, "How could he be a thief? He's Federal . . . a Union soldier, here to preserve the law."

Miss Hennessey tucked her pistol into her reticule and gave a flip to the reins. As the horse started up and they continued their journey she said, "Unfortunately, Peg dear, there are bad apples on both sides."

"I'm sorry he took all your money."

To Peg's surprise Miss Hennessey said, "He didn't take all of it. Only a small amount." She smiled as she said, "Peg, it's time you learned that when women travel alone they carry very little money where it can easily be stolen. I, for one, wrap my traveling money in a handkerchief and pin it inside my corset."

Peg blushed furiously. She had never heard a lady speak of corsets. Ma had said that ladies didn't talk about their undergarments.

"You wondered why I told the sergeant you were my daughter," Miss Hennessey continued.

"Yes, ma'am."

"The members of a Union patrol are trained to look for southern sympathizers or for parties who could be acting against the best interests of the Union."

"Or for spies," Peg added.

"Or for spies," Miss Hennessey repeated. As she turned to look at Peg, for just an instant her gaze seemed troubled. "The patrols interrogate anyone whose behavior is in any way suspicious. Because there has been so much trouble with Missouri bush-whackers, the soldiers are wary. It's certainly accept-able for a mother and daughter to travel together, but if I had said, 'This young woman is a daughter of a friend of mine who agreed to allow her to accompany me,' the soldiers would probably have had further questions and might have insisted on seeing a letter of safe passage for you. We could have been sent back to St. Joseph or even detained. Telling them you were my daughter simplified the entire situation. I didn't think you'd mind."

"I—I don't mind," Peg answered, but she couldn't help feeling a little uncomfortable.

"I can see that the small deception troubles you, even though it's perfectly innocent and can help as-sure our safe travel on this trip and on others."

"On other trips?"

"Yes. If all goes well, you'll be able to visit Danny often. You do understand, don't you, Peg?"

"Yes. Yes, I do!" Peg cried, her heart skipping with excitement.

Miss Hennessey's eyes twinkled as she said, "Then this can be our little secret."

Peg took a sharp breath. "I don't keep secrets from Ma," she said firmly.

"Oh, dear me!" Miss Hennessey reached over and clasped Peg's hand. "I wouldn't dream of asking you to keep secrets from your mother. I'd just like to explain to her in my own way what I told the soldiers and why."

Peg felt a chill, as though a cold breeze had blown across her shoulders. Hadn't Miss Hennessey said almost the same thing after Peg had seen her with her cousin in the woods?

Miss Hennessey and Ma had talked, but Peg hadn't heard the conversation. What exactly had Miss Hennessey told Ma about her cousin? And what was she going to tell her about this?

"You can tell Ma first, if you want," Peg said quietly, "but I'll tell her, too."

"Fair enough," Miss Hennessey said and smiled. She didn't seem to be the least bit bothered by what Peg had said. Peg stared down at her hands, suddenly embarrassed by her concerns, which now appeared to have been silly and childish.

As though nothing out of the ordinary had taken place, Miss Hennessey broke into Peg's thoughts with a happy chirp of a laugh. "Just think, Peg! We're almost at our destination! You'll soon be seeing your brother Danny!"

The excitement in Miss Hennessey's voice was contagious, and Peg's good spirits blossomed. That's why she was here, wasn't it? To see Danny? What did it matter what Miss Hennessey had told the sergeant about her as long as it got them past the patrol? And as for Ma—well, under the circumstances she'd probably agree that what Miss Hennessey had said was sensible and right.

Freed from her worries, Peg eagerly looked forward to surprising Danny.

As they came to a fork in the road Miss Hennessey turned to the left.

Peg waved toward the right. "The Swensons' farm is over there."

"If you don't mind, Peg, we'll stop off at my sister's house first," Miss Hennessey said. "I'm so eager to see Nellie again, and I do so want her to meet you. You're such a delight, and you and your parents have been such dear friends. After a quick hello I'll drive you to see Danny. I promise."

Peg had no choice but to nod agreement, especially when Miss Hennessey added, "I'm so afraid Nellie's feelings would be hurt if she thought you didn't want to meet her."

Within a few moments the road wound up and over a rise and into a clearing in front of a small, trim house. Peg neither saw nor heard signs of any farm animals. Not even a dog came out to greet them.

But, as Miss Hennessey jumped from the buggy and fastened the reins to a hitching post, the front door of the house flew open and a plump, blond woman raced out, her skirts flapping around her legs.

"Violet!" she cried and hugged her sister so enthusiastically she lifted her off her feet.

Peg, who had climbed from the buggy, braced herself as Mrs. Parker stepped back, spied Peg, and descended upon her, arms opened wide.

69

"You must be Peg! Violet wrote about you!"

Peg politely submitted to the hug then looked about for Miss Hennessey.

"She's gone inside to greet my husband," Mrs. Parker said.

Peg took a few steps in the direction of the house, but Mrs. Parker blocked her way. "We'll wait out here," she said.

Even though it was the third of October, it was warm outside in the sun. "I'd like a drink of water, please," Peg said. "If you have a pump in the kitchen . . ."

"The water's cooler at the well," Mrs. Parker said. She took Peg's hand and led her around the side of the house, where she dropped the bucket into the well, then turned the crank to pull it up. Peg picked up the metal cup that rested on the rim of the well and drank deeply. The water *was* cold and tasted delicious. She gulped down the last drop.

A middle-aged, slender man, who wore riding boots, a hat pulled low over his ears, and the dark, homespun clothing worn by many farmers, appeared around the corner of the house. He smiled as he strode toward Peg.

Mrs. Hennessey, who followed behind him, introduced him as Louis Parker.

"I'm pleased to meet you, Mr. Parker," Peg said politely.

He bowed over her hand. "I'm sorry I don't have time for a visit," he said, "but I have a long ride ahead of me. Perhaps next time, Miss Kelly."

Hurried goodbyes were said before he strode to the pasture after his horse.

"Come for a drive with us, Nellie," Miss Hennessey

insisted. "I promised Peg that after the two of you had met, I'd take her immediately to visit her brother."

"Give me one minute to get my bonnet," Mrs. Parker said and ran into the house.

Peg, who had retied her own sunbonnet, sat squeezed between the two laughing, chatting women as Miss Hennessey guided the buggy to the Swensons' farm. Ignoring their lighthearted conversation, which flitted back and forth over her head like butterflies, all Peg could think about was Danny.

The road led through a patch of deep-shaded woodlands and out along low-lying hills. Peg squeaked with delight and bounced on the buggy seat as she finally spotted the familiar two-story house that crowned the top of a rise overlooking the Missouri River. Smoke drifted lazily from the chimney of the kitchen fireplace, and Peg realized—her stomach growling assent—that the Swensons had probably just finished their noon meal.

As Miss Hennessey guided the horse and buggy into the side yard, Peg couldn't wait a second longer. She crawled over Mrs. Parker's lap and leaped to the ground. Running toward the kitchen door she yelled at the top of her lungs, "Danny! Danny!"

The door burst open, and Danny ran out, the alarm on his face quickly changing to a grin as Peg ran to him, her laughter spilling into the sunlight.

"You're taller!" Peg shouted. "No fair, Danny Kelly! You're taller and stronger, and here I thought I'd catch up with you!"

Out of the open door popped Ennie Swenson, her husband Alfrid right behind her. Ennie was as short and plump as ever, Alfrid as tall and lean. Gussie, the hired girl, peeked around the door frame, her eyes wide with curiosity.

Hugs first, or polite introductions? Peg flew into the hugs. The grown-ups could take care of properly meeting one another.

By the time they had introduced themselves, Peg had settled down to just an occasional bounce and a broad smile. She clung to Danny, pulling one hand away only to press it against her stomach as it gave a loud growl.

Bluntly, Gussie said, "Girl, I bet your last meal was breakfast, and who knows how long it's been since then? Come with me, and I'll fix you a plate."

"Miss Hennessey, Mrs. Parker, we have some cold chicken," Ennie quickly offered, but Miss Hennessey shook her head.

"You're very kind, but we'll decline your generous invitation. I know you have much to talk about with Peg, and Nellie and I have to catch up on all the years we've been apart."

"Years?" Ennie asked.

"Yes, four," Mrs. Parker said, while at the same time Miss Hennessey answered, "Five."

Mrs. Parker rolled her eyes and giggled. "Oh, dear, has it really been that long, Violet? I seem to have lost all track of time."

Miss Hennessey smiled at Peg. "I'll be back to pick you up at three o'clock," she told her.

"Thank you. I'll be ready," Peg answered politely, although her attention had been captured by the fragrant odors wafting from the open kitchen door.

She didn't wait to watch Miss Hennessey and her sister drive away. She raced into the kitchen, tugging Danny with her, and dove into the nearest chair. Ennie's chicken was good, hot or cold; the baked yellow squash, with butter and a touch of cinnamon, was still warm, and the apple dumpling Gussie set before her rivaled Ma's.

After welcoming Peg again, Alfrid said, "Danny, I can easily finish our fence mending by myself. You stay here and visit with Peg. Look how glad she is to see you. Or could it be Ennie's apple dumplings that have Peg so excited?"

"The dumplings, of course," Peg said and grinned at Danny.

As Alfrid left, Ennie served Danny and Peg second helpings of the dumplings, then plopped into a chair at the table. "So the Parkers are living on the Millers' place," she said to Peg. "I hear they didn't buy the land but are only renting. Thad and Gennie Miller moved out west, you know, after their second son was killed."

Peg swallowed noisily, sure of what Ma'd have to say if she talked with her mouth full. Trying her best to remember the Millers, she said, "No, I'm sorry. I didn't know."

"It was after the raids last year," Ennie said. "Union patrols suspected the Millers of having southern sympathies and arrested their son, Joshua. Amos, the younger son, was so upset he ran off and joined the bushwhackers."

Danny spoke up. "Then they *were* southern sympathizers."

"Some said *yes*, some said *no*. I, myself, never thought so," Ennie said with a sigh. "But then, nowadays, who knows? How many people, loyal to the Union, changed their allegiance because of the cruelty of those Union patrols?"

"The bushwhackers are cruel, too," Danny insisted.

"That's right," Ennie said. "They've done horrible things to many innocent people. These are hard times for all of us. I can only pray that they'll soon be over."

As she smoothed her apron across her ample lap, a smile brightened her features. "No more talk of war," she said. "Let's talk about pleasant things. How is your mother, Peg?"

"Fine," Peg said. She drank a long gulp from the glass of sweet milk Gussie had placed before her, then wiped off her damp milk mustache with the back of one hand.

"And you, dear? Is all going well with you?"

"Yes, ma'am," Peg answered.

"You're growing up to be a lovely young lady, Peg."

"Thank you," Peg said. She looked at the large bite of apple on her fork, put it back into the bowl and cut it into a daintier piece—the size a young lady would eat.

Ennie leaned toward her, eyes twinkling with curiosity. "Tell me about Miss Hennessey," she said.

Peg looked up, surprised. "You just met her."

"She certainly seems very pleasant," Ennie began. "Your mother has never mentioned Miss Hennessey. How long has she known her? Where did she come from?"

Peg thought a moment. She'd have an eager audience if she told Ennie in great detail about Miss Hennessey's flight from Quantrill's raiders and Frances Mary bringing her to St. Joe and shelter at their home. But the apple dumpling was gone, her stomach was full, and she'd rather spend her short time here with Danny.

She tried to remember Ennie's questions as she answered, "Ma hasn't known Miss Hennessey for very long . . . just a couple of weeks. She lives in St. Joe, and she comes from Boston."

"Don't you know anything about her family?"

Peg stared in surprise. "Her sister's name is Nellie Parker, and she was here just a few minutes ago."

Ennie sighed and hoisted herself from her chair. "Never mind," she said and gave her apron a shake. "Why don't you children run outside and play?"

Peg tried not to look as aggrieved as she felt. Not more than fifteen minutes ago Ennie Swenson had called Peg a young lady, yet now she was sounding just like Ma! Peg tossed back her shoulders and tried to look as old as she felt.

Danny grabbed Peg's arm, jerked her to her feet, and propelled her out the back door. He didn't stop until they had reached the field behind the barn.

"Stop that!" Peg pulled away with such force she lost her balance and flopped onto the grass.

Danny dropped down beside her. "Then don't act so prissy in front of Ennie."

"I wasn't prissy."

"You were, too. You should have seen your face."

Peg's lower lip curled into a pout. "She said we were children."

"You are a child. You're only eleven."

"Eleven's almost grown-up."

"It is not."

"Is too." Peg broke off a handful of grass, enjoying the stinging, sour fragrance as it tickled her nose. Laughing, she threw it at Danny.

Puzzled when he didn't laugh, too, Peg demanded, "What's the matter with you?"

Danny's face was serious as he looked at Peg. "I could tell that you didn't want to spend a lot of time gossiping with Ennie about Miss Hennessey," Danny said. "But if you do know something about her, you have to tell me what it is."

Taken by surprise, Peg could only blurt out, "Why?"

"The Miller house . . . the Parker house now . . . there's something strange going on there."

Peg leaned close, a little frightened by the seriousness in Danny's voice. "What something strange?" she whispered.

"Ennie sent me over to the Parkers with one of her cakes and a bowl of eggs when they first moved in," Danny said, "and I've ridden nearby a couple of times since . . . near enough to see, that is."

Peg grabbed his arm, exasperated that it was taking him so long to explain. "See what? Tell me, Danny!"

"The Parkers live on a farm," he said, "so by rights they should work it. But they're not farming. They don't have animals, and they're not growing crops. How can they manage to survive on a farm if they don't work it?"

Peg tried to remember all that Miss Hennessey had said. "They're not staying long. It's just . . . just temporary."

"That doesn't make sense. If they're in these parts for a short time, then why not stay in town?"

"I don't know," Peg said.

"Maybe there are things about the Parkers and Miss Hennessey we *should* know. Our Union's at war." Danny tried to look serious, but his scowl soon dissolved into a grin. "I mean it, Peg," he said. "You and I could find out."

"How? By asking questions?"

Danny nodded. "And by keeping our eyes and ears open."

Peg took a sharp breath. "Do you mean spying?"

"Not the I-Spy-peeking-around-the-corner games that little children do."

Peg's face grew warm, and she quickly looked away. Just a few weeks ago she and May had been playing spying on Marcus.

But Danny hadn't noticed Peg's embarrassment. "I mean carefully watching and listening to find out what the Parkers might be up to." He looked at Peg intently. "Do you think you could do it?"

Peg sat up a little taller. "Of course," she said. "I'm not a child."

"Then tell," Danny said. "How much do you know about Miss Hennessey?"

9

PEG LAY BACK on the soft grass, letting the sunshine seep through her skin and warm her bones. She had promised Danny to find out what she could about the Parkers and Miss Hennessey, and now he wanted her to tell everything she already had learned. But what did she really know that she could tell? Miss Hennessey had been a guest in their home—quiet and shy, but friendly—and Ma trusted her.

Her suspicions were only that—suspicions, with no proof behind them. How could she tell Danny about Miss Hennessey's cousin, who was one of Quantrill's raiders? Or about the deception under which Miss Hennessey and she were traveling as mother and daughter? Miss Hennessey had given Peg perfectly good explanations, and Peg had decided to accept them. But would Danny? What if he insisted on being the big, protective brother and suspiciously jumped to the wrong conclusions?

"If all goes well, you'll be able to visit Danny often," Miss Hennessey had said.

Everything has to go well! It has to! Peg told herself. *What does it matter that the Parkers don't have farm animals? What difference does it make if they live on a farm or in town? Who knows? Who cares? I'm not going to let silly suspicions spoil my trips to see Danny!*

A fistful of grass blades landed on Peg's face. She sat up, shaking her head, and sneezed.

"Well?" Danny asked. "What can you tell me about Miss Hennessey?"

"She's nice," Peg said.

"That's all?"

"That's all. Ma likes her, and so do I." Trying to ignore the small but growing guilt that made her stomach ache, Peg scrambled to her feet. "Come on, Danny," she said and held out a hand. "Let's run down to the river. I can skip stones farther than you can!"

Danny stood, and Peg was surprised once again at how fast he had grown. "I bet you're taller than Mike now," she said.

"I was already taller by an inch when he came through St. Joe two years ago." Danny suddenly grinned and said, "I've got a better idea than skipping stones. I set up targets at the edge of the woods. I'll show you what a good shot I am."

Peg reluctantly trailed after Danny as he got his rifle from the house and led her to the practice area. "You don't have to show me," she complained. "I believe you."

"I'm really good," he bragged. "I want you to see."

Danny found Peg a place to stand, behind him and

far enough away so that the crack of the rifle wouldn't hurt her ears. He raised his rifle and sighted on a tattered round-ringed target that had been nailed onto the broad trunk of an oak tree.

"Take that, you bushwhackers!" Danny grunted and squeezed the trigger.

Peg watched a small piece of cloth near the center of the target rip as the bullet struck it. Sickened, she clutched her stomach.

Danny turned to face her, pride shining in his eyes. "Got him!" he said. "One less Reb."

"Don't do that, Danny!" Peg shouted. "It's only a target! It's not a Reb!"

"Someday it will be a Reb," Danny said. "As soon as I enlist to fight for the Union."

"You can forget that!" Peg insisted. "You're not going to shoot Rebs! You're not going to war!"

"I'm older than Mike was when he enlisted."

"He was too young! He's still too young. And so are you."

"I won't be thirteen forever."

"The war's going to end soon. Everybody says so."

"Then everybody's dreaming."

"Oh, Danny!" Peg wailed. Maybe it was her own fear. Maybe it was remembering Mike's eyes when he returned from battle. But like a dark spirit that hovered over Danny, a terrible premonition caught and shook her. "If you go to war you'll be killed! I know it! You will!"

Danny sighed. "I wouldn't have brought you here if I'd known you'd act like such a baby. Don't you see, Peg? I have a duty to my country. I love the Union. I want to help protect it."

"But not by fighting!"

"Yes, by fighting."

"But there are other ways to help the Union."

"You don't understand," Danny said. He turned his back to her, reloaded his rifle, and aimed once again at the target.

Peg watched in misery as the bullet hit its mark. *"You don't understand,"* Danny had said, ignoring all that she'd told him. What had happened to Danny, who'd always been so close to her? He'd built a wall without a door, and she couldn't come through. Hugging her shoulders, Peg waited silently until Danny had finished his show of marksmanship.

"You have to admit I'm a good shot," he said.

Peg nodded. "Yes, you are."

Carrying his rifle in the crook of one arm, Danny grinned and put his other arm around Peg's shoulders. As they walked back toward the house he squinted up at the sun and said, "It should be near to three o'clock. Miss Hennessey will come to get you before long."

Peg leaned close to him, frantic that the time was almost up. "I'll be back soon," she said. "Miss Hennessey will invite me to travel with her again when she comes to visit her sister. She promised."

"Good!" Giving her shoulder a squeeze, Danny said, "Because of the Union patrols, Buchanan County's been quiet lately. While you were on the road you probably met up with a patrol, didn't you?"

"One," Peg said and turned her face so that Danny couldn't see her eyes. "Miss Hennessey had a letter of safe passage given to her by our provost marshal, so the sergeant let us through."

I can't tell Danny the rest of what happened, Peg thought. *He wouldn't understand.* With a start she realized that she had built a wall, too—a wall that she wouldn't allow Danny to break through.

"We've heard that the patrols have been hard on

some of the people who resisted when Missouri was put under martial law," Danny said, "but they keep down the bushwhackers—at least, they have locally. I hear there are still plenty of skirmishes in southern Missouri, especially in the border counties."

There was so much pride in Danny's voice as he spoke of the Union patrols that Peg was glad she hadn't told him about the soldier who had stolen Miss Hennessey's money. She doubted that Danny would even believe it had happened.

Peg scarcely had time to brush the grass and tangles from her hair and securely tie on her sunbonnet before Miss Hennessey arrived.

They left with a carton containing two jars of Ennie's special sweet cucumber pickles, a sack of fresh eggs, and a fat loaf cake.

"Give these to your dear mother with my greatest affection," Ennie told Peg, who tried not to grin. Peg had no doubt that Ennie really did like Ma, but wasn't that only because Alfrid had married Ennie, instead of following the plan Peg and Danny had once worked out to bring Ma west as Alfrid's bride?

On the return trip Miss Hennessey seemed happier and more relaxed. "It did me a world of good to see my sister again," she told Peg. "Nellie hasn't changed a bit. She's always so cheerful, no matter how difficult things may be."

"You mean like not having any livestock?" Peg blurted out.

"I told you their stay in this area will be short."

Embarrassed, Peg's face grew hot. "I know. It's just that, well, on a farm I expected a dog to run out to meet us, and one didn't, so then I listened, and I couldn't hear chickens, and . . ."

As Peg's voice trailed away Miss Hennessey nodded. "You're very observant and you're right. Louis once had a fine house and good stock, but he has no plans to farm again—at least not until the war is over."

"Was his livestock stolen?"

"Yes, and his house burned."

"I'm sorry."

"I'm sorry, too, but I'm grateful that their lives were spared."

"Where were they when this happened?"

"In southern Missouri, near the Arkansas border."

"Bushwhackers?"

"Yes. One of the rebel gangs." A note of bitterness crept into Miss Hennessey's voice. "In Missouri it's hard to be pro-Union, and it's hard to be pro-southern. If it's not the bushwhackers, it's the military patrols."

Peg squirmed on the buggy seat, wishing it were softer. "Why don't your sister and her husband leave Missouri?"

"They will, some day." She sighed before she answered, "I'll go, too. Maybe to California . . . I've always wanted to see San Francisco."

As the horse and buggy clopped and clattered around a bend, through the trees Peg caught a quick glimpse of Union blue. "A patrol!" she whispered. "Just up ahead."

"Thank you," Miss Hennessey answered calmly. She flicked the horse's reins, her hands firm and back straight, as though nothing out of the ordinary could possibly happen, and continued chatting to Peg; but her voice changed to the same light conversational tone that some of Ma's friends used when they stopped by for a cup of tea.

"I understand that San Francisco is a vital, energetic town with great potential for trade by both sea and rail," she said.

But all Peg could think about was the little silvery handgun hidden in Miss Hennessey's reticule and the bearded soldier who had stolen some of Miss Hennessey's money.

Peg tensed as the sound of horses' hooves increased and the patrol rode into view, but she sighed with relief when she saw it was a different group of soldiers. The bearded thief was nowhere in sight.

Miss Hennessey obediently pulled the horse to a stop on the patrol leader's orders and smiled at him. "My daughter and I have a letter of safe passage from General John Bassett," she said. "Would you like to see it, Sergeant?"

"Corporal," he barked. As she reached into her reticule, he said, "Just hand over your bag, ma'am. I'll get the letter myself."

"As you wish," Miss Hennessey said. She immediately handed him the reticule, but Peg held her breath. *The gun! He was going to discover the gun!*

The corporal's fingers explored the small bag, but he pulled out the letter, not the handgun. Peg's breath came out in a whoosh of relief. Obviously, the handgun wasn't in the reticule. Where was it?

The corporal squinted, and his lips moved as he slowly read the letter. "From what I can make out," he finally said, "you live in St. Joe and have been down to River Road to see your sister."

"That's correct," Miss Hennessey said. She smiled at him shyly.

He folded the letter and stuck it back inside the reticule, handing it to Miss Hennessey.

We can go now! Peg thought with relief. Even though she was Union, too, as were most of their friends in St. Joe, Peg had had enough of Union patrols.

But one of the soldiers had leaned from his horse to peer into the buggy. "Box of something back here," he said to the corporal.

As he pushed at the box Peg shouted, "Watch out for the eggs! They'll break!"

"Ma'am, you and your little girl climb down from the buggy," the corporal said. "We're goin' to do a search. Nothin' special. It's routine."

"A search for what?" Miss Hennessey asked.

The corporal didn't answer. As she stood by the buggy with Miss Hennessey, Peg watched with wide eyes as one soldier examined every single egg, accidentally cracking two of them. As he opened the pickle jars and plunged his fingers inside, Peg grimaced in disgust. She'd been looking forward to munching on the sweet, crispy pickles, but now she wouldn't touch them! Two of the soldiers crawled in and out of the buggy, examining the seats, the canopy, and even the underside. Another soldier checked the trappings on the horse. What if Miss Hennessey had hidden her gun somewhere in the buggy? The soldiers would find it!

But they came up empty.

"Perhaps I could help you, if you'd only tell me the purpose of your search," Miss Hennessey said.

But without a word, the corporal motioned to her to get back into the buggy. When she and Peg had seated themselves, he handed Miss Hennessey the reins and said, "You can go now."

Stirring up a choking cloud of dust, the soldiers dug their boots into their horses' flanks and galloped off.

Peg squinted and rubbed the dust from her eyes. "I thought they'd find your gun," she said.

Miss Hennessey smiled. "I realized I had been reckless in keeping it inside my reticule," she told Peg. "It's safely tucked into the pocket of my skirt."

Peg twisted to look down the road in the direction the soldiers had ridden. "What will we do if one of them rides back to rob you, like last time?"

"I don't think we'll have that problem again."

Peg settled back and began to relax. "What were they looking for?"

"The corporal wouldn't tell us," Miss Hennessey answered.

"Can you guess?"

Miss Hennessey stared straight ahead, her eyes on the road, as she answered, "I haven't the vaguest idea."

Peg stole a quick glance at Miss Hennessey's profile, which was calm and impassive and told her nothing. Miss Hennessey's answer had made perfect sense. Peg had heard her ask the corporal why the buggy was being searched.

So why, Peg wondered, did she have the strange feeling that Miss Hennessey *did* know what the soldiers were looking for?

10

MA WAS ELATED with Ennie Swenson's gifts, until Peg blurted out, "Don't eat the pickles. One of the soldiers in a Union patrol stuck his dirty, grimy hand in them."

"For goodness sakes, why?" Ma asked. She stared at the jar of pickles as though something awful were about to lift the lid and spring out.

Miss Hennessey chuckled indulgently. "He was a very young, overly conscientious corporal, who was probably looking for something sinister like smuggled-out lists of troop dispatchments. Would you believe his soldiers actually searched the buggy?"

Ma was about to speak, but Miss Hennessey quickly said, "But I'm grateful for the patrols on the road. We met up with one going and another one coming. Thanks to the presence of our Union soldiers I felt perfectly safe."

"Yes," Ma said, but she didn't look entirely convinced. The kettle began steaming, so Ma took it from the fire and filled the teapot.

Miss Hennessey pulled out a kitchen chair and sat down. Elbows on the table, she rested her chin in her hands as she said, "The sergeant of the first patrol was an unlettered man. I could tell he was going to follow every rule in the book, down to the smallest detail. The way he frowned as he read General Bassett's letter of safe passage, then studied Peg, alerted me to the fact that he was going to demand a similar letter for Peg."

She reached for the cup of tea Ma handed her and sighed. "All I could think was that we'd be turned back, and after all this time I wouldn't see my sister Nellie. I was frantic!" She leaned toward Ma. "What would you have done, Noreen?"

"Well," Ma said, taken by surprise. "I—I suppose I would have tried to explain, and—"

"An explanation wouldn't have meant anything to a man like that. If it weren't listed in the rules he'd memorized, he wouldn't have known what to do with it."

Again, Miss Hennessey paused and waited for Ma to speak.

Flustered, Ma began, "Then I might have . . . uh . . ."

"I'm sure you would have done what I did," Miss Hennessey said. "I told the sergeant that Peg was my daughter. That satisfied him, and we were allowed to proceed."

"I suppose in a case like that—"

Miss Hennessey interrupted, a broad smile on her face. "Oh, Noreen, how I wish I really did have a daughter like Peg. She's such a dear, lovely young woman and a pleasant traveling companion."

Peg blushed, but didn't speak. She was too busy thinking over what Miss Hennessey had told Ma about misleading the soldiers into thinking that Peg was Miss Hennessey's daughter. She'd kept her promise to tell, in her own way, just as she'd said she would, so Peg couldn't complain; but her *own way* was just a tad different from the way Peg would have told Ma. At least Miss Hennessey's deception got her past the patrol and to Danny, so did the way the story was told really matter?

Miss Hennessey pushed back her chair and got to her feet. "I know that you have dozens of questions to ask about Danny," she said, "and I'm sure Peg can't wait to tell you about the happy afternoon they spent together. So I'll leave now with my grateful thanks." She paused. "I do hope you'll allow Peg to drive with me again."

"Please, Ma! Please, please?" Peg waited eagerly for Ma's answer.

"Since you feel it's safe enough," Ma said. Her eyes were warm with affection as she looked at Peg.

The moment Miss Hennessey's buggy had left Ma wrapped an arm around Peg's waist and steered her to the sofa. "Tell me about Danny, little love," she said.

Peg sighed. *"Little love"* again. Why couldn't Ma think of her as a young lady? Miss Hennessey did.

But Peg soon forgot her grievance in her delight in telling Ma how tall and strong Danny was growing. Smiling, Ma asked question after question, and Peg answered as best she could, but she didn't tell Ma about Danny's target practice and his eagerness to enlist in the Union Army as soon as he'd reached the age of sixteen. Why worry Ma about something that might never happen? Surely the war would be over by then.

Surprising Peg, Ma suddenly asked, "Tell me about

Miss Hennessey's sister Nellie and her husband. Are they friendly, good people? Is Nellie as shy as Violet is?"

"She's very different," Peg answered. "She gives huge, squashing hugs, and she laughs a lot. She doesn't even look like Miss Hennessey."

At Ma's urging, Peg went on to describe the poor, impoverished farm that still lacked livestock. "But they're only going to be there temporarily," Peg said.

"The poor dears," Ma said and slowly shook her head. "War causes such terrible waste."

With a rush of affection Peg snuggled up against Ma. "Come with us next time. Please? Danny would love to see you."

"Maybe," Ma said, "although it's hard for me to leave my chores and get away. Who'd tend to John when he came home from his shop? Who'd cook his dinner?"

"Who cooked it before he married you?" Peg demanded.

Ma grinned and gave Peg a playful squeeze. "Don't be saucy."

"Think about coming with us, will you, Ma?" Peg begged.

"Do you know when Violet plans to make the drive again?"

"No," Peg said. "I just hope it's soon."

A few days later John came home with a copy of *The St. Joseph Gazette* and thumped it onto the table. "That monster, William Quantrill, should be drawn and quartered!"

Ma exclaimed, "John Murphy, I'm surprised at you!"

He sank into the nearest kitchen chair and rubbed

his neck. "You look tired," Peg told him. "Would you like a drink of water?"

"I'm just discouraged, Peg, my girl, after reading the news," he said.

"What happened?" Peg poured water into a cup for him, then reached for the newspaper, but Ma was quicker and snatched it up.

"John," she said, "suppose you give us the essence of the story. Just remember to leave out the worst of the details."

He nodded. "On October first, Quantrill called his men to meet in the town of Perdees, in Johnson County. Four hundred of them showed up. The plan was to ride south along the Kansas-Missouri border into Arkansas and then down into Texas, where they'd stay the winter."

Peg thought about James, Miss Hennessey's cousin. Had he known he'd be going to Texas? And when he'd said he'd soon have word, did he mean that to be the date they'd be going?

John looked glum as he continued the story. "As they neared our Fort Baxter, on the sixth, Quantrill decided to attack. Fortunately, Quantrill's troops were beaten back."

"Then the news isn't so bad," Ma said, and Peg could hear the relief in her voice.

"I'm not through with the telling," Mr. Murphy said. He gave a long sigh, drank half the water Peg had put before him, and finally continued: "The Union commander of the District of the Frontier, General James Blunt, was traveling on his way from Fort Scott to Fort Gibson. There were ten wagons in his train along with one hundred men of the Third Wisconsin and Fourteenth Kansas Cavalry. And a woman traveled with them—Mrs. Chester Thomas, the wife of an army contractor, who was on the way to join her husband.

"Quantrill was informed that the train was approaching, so he and two hundred and fifty of his men rode out to meet it. Some of Quantrill's men were dressed partially in Union uniforms, so General Blunt decided that they were an honor guard sent from Fort Baxter to greet him. He led his party right into the ambush."

"How awful!" Peg exclaimed.

Ma clapped her hands to her cheeks. "What happened to them? And to that poor woman?"

"General Blunt and Mrs. Thomas jumped from their buggy onto horses and were able to escape. A few others escaped as well, but there were many, many casualties.

John's face twisted in anguish. "The victory must have lit a bonfire inside Quantrill. As he and his men continued below Baxter Springs, they killed one hundred and fifty Indians and Negroes who were gathering ponies for the Union Army."

"Oh, mercy, mercy!" Ma said as she wiped her hands on her apron. "Peg, you shouldn't be hearing all this."

"Yes, I should," Peg insisted. "I'm not a small child. It's better that I know what is happening."

"I agree," John said. "You can't hide Peg inside a bushel barrel."

Miffed, Ma insisted, "That may be, but for now let there be no more talk about war."

"But I have a question," Peg said. "There's something I don't understand. If Quantrill was told that General Blunt's train of wagons was coming, then why wasn't there someone to tell General Blunt that Quantrill's raiders were traveling south?"

John frowned. "You have a good point. The Union has as many spies as the Confederates. By all rights the general should have been told."

"That's what I mean. Why wasn't he?"

"Who knows? There may have been a spy rushing the information to the general. If the spy was male and he was caught by some of the bushwhackers, he would have been shot—or possibly hanged on the spot."

"Now, John," Ma said with an anxious look toward Peg.

But Peg persisted. "What do you mean—if the spy was male? Aren't all spies hanged?"

"No. If the spy was a woman she would have been imprisoned, but she wouldn't have been killed. Neither side kills women. Even Quantrill doesn't kill women."

Peg was intrigued. "Then why not make a rule that all spies have to be women?"

"Because there are some places women just can't go."

"But if—"

Ma slammed the palm of her hand on the table. "That's enough! Supper is ready, and there'll be only talk of pleasant things while we're at the table. Is that understood?"

As John left to wash up, Peg glanced at the bowl of pickles Ma had placed on the table along with a small boiled sausage, turnips, and mashed potatoes. "Ma," she asked, "Those aren't Ennie Swenson's pickles, are they?"

"It's wrong to throw away perfectly good pickles," Ma said with a warning frown that told Peg she'd better not pursue the topic. "Eat them and enjoy them. Believe me, I scrubbed them well."

Before Peg fell asleep that night, she thought about

Miss Hennessey's cousin, James. Quantrill and his men hadn't been in battle when they'd ambushed the general's wagon train and when they'd ridden down on the Indians and Negroes. They'd slaughtered people who were not prepared to fight back. Cousin, or not, how could James do such a thing?

Miss Hennessey must read the newspaper. What would she think? How terrible must she feel?

I'll go to see her tomorrow after school, Peg promised herself. Lazily she curled and uncurled her toes in the warm cocoon created by the down quilt, and soon she was fast asleep.

In spite of her determination, the next day Peg didn't go to see Miss Hennessey. Black clouds swept down from the Northwest, and a brisk wind blew the icy rain in gusts that soaked the passersby who had to stagger through the storm.

"Miss Hennessey will keep," Ma said, as she stripped off Peg's wet clothes in the kitchen and wrapped Peg in towels she'd heated in the oven. "With a storm like this, she's going nowhere, and neither are you."

"But it's important."

"Just why is it so important?"

Tentatively, Peg said, "Her cousin James. After what was in the newspaper about Quantrill . . . Miss Hennessey may feel badly."

"I shouldn't wonder," Ma said. "I'd forgotten about the bad apple of her family who rides with Quantrill. Well, your going out in the rain isn't going to help Violet or you, and it may put you in your bed, if you catch cold."

She did tell Ma! She promised she would, and she

did! Giddy with relief, Peg said, "I'll see her tomorrow, then."

"Not if this weather holds."

And the weather did, the skies not breaking clear until late Friday afternoon.

Ma sighed as she held up the coat Peg flung on the chair the moment she returned from school. "Can you tell me, missy, how the back of your coat came to be splattered with mud?"

"It was Marcus's fault," Peg muttered. "He got me with two mud balls. I told him that when I caught him I'd rub mud in his face and pour it down the back of his shirt." She scowled. "If I could have caught him, I would have."

Quickly changing her mood, Peg peered out the kitchen window and said, "The rain's gone, Ma. Could I go and see Miss Hennessey now?"

"In this coat? Covered in mud?" Ma emphatically shook her head. "And I'm sure if you caught sight of your friend Marcus on the way, you'd have even more mud to account for."

"He's not my friend, Ma, and besides—"

"We'll hang the coat to dry," Ma said, "and with a good, hard brushing tomorrow, we should get rid of the mud. Perhaps you can visit Miss Hennessey then."

Eager for the next day to arrive, Peg woke before the others and took care of the kitchen chores so breakfast could be made. One pan sizzled with sliced potatoes, and another with eggs.

When Ma came downstairs, she gave Peg a broad smile. "What a good, helpful girl you are, love," she said.

"As soon as I finish my chores, may I visit Miss Hennessey?" Peg asked.

Ma laughed. "Just give the poor woman time to

wake up." She took Peg's coat and a stiff brush out in the backyard and returned with an only slightly stained coat. While Peg sliced the bread, Ma worked on the stains with a damp rag.

"Almost good as new," she said. "Just stay away from Marcus Hurd. Maybe I should have a talk with his mother."

Peg shook her head and smiled. On such a beautiful, sunlit day she couldn't feel upset at anyone—even Marcus.

Soon after John had left for his blacksmith's shop, while Peg was washing the breakfast dishes and Ma was collecting the week's dirty laundry, Violet Hennessey arrived. The moment Peg heard the clip-clop of the horse's hooves and the creak of buggy wheels she raced to the front door and threw it open.

Miss Hennessey, dressed in a somber dark gray traveling coat and hat, was pale, and the skin around her eyes was dark. "I had no way to get in touch with you earlier," she said. "Only this morning I received word that Nellie's husband, Louis, has been hurt. I must go to them, and I hope to stay the night. Please, may Peg travel with me?"

"Violet! How dreadful!" Ma cried. Without pausing for breath, she spoke quickly, her words tripping over each other. "What happened to Louis? How was he hurt? How *badly* was he hurt? Does he need a doctor? Is there anything I can do to help?"

Miss Hennessey blindly groped for the sturdy back of the wing chair and sank into it. "Louis was shot," she said.

Ma and Peg gasped, but Miss Hennessey said, "It was in his right arm, but the bullet went through cleanly, and the bone was not broken. He's feverish, but Nellie wrote that he's improving and she's sure he'll survive."

Glancing with a worried look from Miss Hennessey to Peg, Ma asked, *"Where* did this happen?"

"Oh, dear me! Please don't get the wrong impression!" Miss Hennessey's hands fluttered as she explained, "It was *not* at their farm. Louis was riding through southern Missouri on business."

"Southern Missouri is dangerous country," Ma said. "I've heard that most of the farms close to the Kansas border have been abandoned."

The Kansas border? Peg remembered what her stepfather had told them. "Was it Quantrill who shot him?" Peg blurted out. "He and his raiders were moving south."

Miss Hennessey gave a start. "No! It wasn't Quantrill!" She took a deep breath, forced herself to calm down, and answered, "According to what Louis told Nellie, there was only a single attacker, whose purpose must have been to rob Louis. Fortunately, Louis was able to ride faster and farther, leaving his pursuer behind."

Miss Hennessey sighed. "There was no one who could have helped Louis. We are grateful he was able to make the long ride home."

Ma patted Miss Hennessey's shoulder and asked, "Can I send any medicine with you? I have a tonic that works well for chills and fever, and I can quickly make up a poultice for the chest."

"Thank you," Miss Hennessey said, "but I'm sure that Nellie has enough of the proper remedies. It's Peg I want. I doubt if I have the strength or the courage to travel alone."

Ma thought in silence, while Peg held her breath.

"Very well," she finally said. "You'll have her home before tomorrow evening?"

Miss Hennessey smiled. "Safe and sound," she said.

"I'll run upstairs and get ready!" Peg cried. *Safe and sound*, she repeated to herself, but as she fumbled with the buttons on her dress her fingers trembled.

11

BUNDLED UP AGAINST the crisp air, Peg tried to spark interesting conversations, commenting on the beauty of the red and gold leaves of fall, Ma's receipt for apple custard pie, and even the disastrous results of Marcus Hurd's hiding a dead frog in Miss Thomas's desk; but Miss Hennessey's thoughts seemed to be far away. Finally, becoming as silent as her companion, Peg wistfully remembered their previous trip and Miss Hennessey's good humor.

Granted, it was terrible that Louis Parker had been shot, but he was recovering, wasn't he? Nellie had written so. Ma had sent with them a large jar of barley soup and two loaves of bread, which should make anyone feel better. Why was Miss Hennessey so deeply depressed?

When they were close to River Road a patrol approached, and for the first time Miss Hennessey sat up smartly.

"Don't tell them about Louis," she ordered Peg, who felt somewhat aggrieved that Miss Hennessey hadn't taken it for granted that she was old enough to know better.

As the soldiers—none of whom they'd seen before —stopped beside the buggy, Miss Hennessey smiled and handed their patrol leader her letter of safe passage. "My daughter and I are paying a visit to my sister," she said.

This soldier seemed less interested in them than had the other two patrol leaders they'd met. "What's in the box?" he asked as he handed back the letter.

"Two loaves of bread and a container of barley soup," Miss Hennessey answered.

"And the carpetbags?"

"A change of clothing."

With a lazy wave of his hand he said, "Go on your way." He rode on, his men following, not even looking back to see if Miss Hennessey had obeyed.

As they reached River Road Miss Hennessey pulled the horse's reins to the right.

"Aren't we going to your sister's house?" Peg asked.

"There's no need to bring you there," Miss Hennessey said. "I'll take you to the Swensons' and pick you up tomorrow afternoon about three."

"You won't need me to help take care of Mr. Parker?"

For the first time Miss Hennessey smiled. "No, dear. As I told you and your mother, Nellie wrote that Louis is improving. He'll need rest more than anything else."

Peg's heart jumped with delight. She'd be free to

spend both days with Danny. A small pang of guilt caused her to say, "You're sure you won't need me?"

"I'm sure."

The moment the buggy halted, Peg thanked Miss Hennessey, snatched her small carpetbag, and leaped to the ground.

When Ennie, who had heard the buggy arrive, came out to greet Miss Hennessey, Peg grabbed her around the waist and cried, "I can stay until tomorrow afternoon!" Remembering her manners, she calmed down enough to add, "If you'll have me, that is."

"Of course we will," Ennie said, "but you'll find that Danny has a bit of a sniffle and cough and is tucked in bed with a mustard plaster on his chest. He *would* go out in that dreadful rainstorm that blew through here."

Peg didn't wait to hear any more. She left Ennie chatting with Miss Hennessey and ran into the Swensons' house. Peg knew where Danny's room was, and she knew she'd be staying in her old bedroom, so she threw her coat and carpetbag on her bed and raced to Danny's bedroom, next door.

"We're being attacked!" Danny yelled, as Peg banged on the closed door and slammed it open at the same time.

Peg grinned. "I'm here for two days this time!"

"All of you?"

"What do you mean, *all* of me?"

Danny pushed himself to a sitting position. "You made enough noise for ten people. I was sure a passel of bushwhackers was after me."

Peg made a face as she flounced onto the end of Danny's bed. "Phew! You stink!" she said.

Danny held the top of his nightshirt away from his body. "Mostly, all I've got is a runny nose, but Ennie insisted on a mustard plaster the first time she heard me cough. The smelly thing's about to burn a hole in my chest."

Peg studied Danny. "She's probably right. Your nose is red, and you've left soggy handkerchiefs—ugh! —all over the floor. Why'd you go out in the rainstorm if you didn't have to?"

Danny didn't answer. He listened intently, his eyes on the hall, then whispered, "Peg, close the door, and be quiet about it. There's something I've got to tell you."

Peg did as Danny said, then returned to perch on the foot of his bed. She wasn't used to seeing such deep concern in Danny's eyes, and it frightened her a little. "What's the matter?" she asked.

Bluntly, Danny said, "Your Miss Hennessey's brother-in-law, Mr. Parker, was shot in the arm."

"I know that. It's why Miss Hennessey came today to visit the Parkers. Mr. Parker was set upon by a robber, but he managed to get away, made it home by himself, and he's already improving."

"There you go, getting prissy again," Danny complained. "You don't know everything. Did Miss Hennessey tell you that story about a robber?"

"Yes. And it's not a story. It's what really happened."

"I don't think so, Peg," Danny said.

"What are you talking about?"

"Tell me exactly what Miss Hennessey said, and then I'll explain what I mean."

"All right." Peg thought hard, trying to remember the exact words, before she answered. "Louis was shot in the right arm, but it was a clean wound and it didn't break the bone."

"Where did it happen?"

"South of here, near the Kansas border." Peg hesitated. "I asked if he was shot by Quantrill, and Miss Hennessey said he wasn't."

"That's a strange question. Why'd you happen to ask that?"

"Because John Murphy had read to us about Quantrill's men getting together near the Kansas border and riding south, heading for Texas."

Danny frowned. "I read that, too. Do you know the rest?"

"Yes," Peg said. "I know Quantrill and his raiders stopped to attack a fort, but they didn't win, so they attacked a general and his wagon train and then went on to kill some Indians and Negroes who were rounding up ponies for the Union Army."

"How'd Quantrill know the wagon train was coming?"

"Somebody told him, I guess." Peg frowned. "And somebody should have told that Union general where Quantrill's men were."

"It looks like the Confederates had spies and the Federals didn't."

"It's not fair!" Peg huffed.

"It's never going to be," Danny answered.

Peg suddenly remembered what Danny had said earlier. "You didn't tell me what you meant. You said that the story about a robbery was just a story."

"At least some of it, maybe all of it."

"Why?"

"Pay attention, and I'll tell you. I was near the River Road on Thursday, rounding up two stray cows before the storm broke, and saw Mr. Parker ride home. Another man rode with him, which was lucky for Mr. Parker, I guess, because Mr. Parker was all bent over and looked something terrible."

"Miss Hennessey said he made it home alone."

"He didn't. I followed them. That's how I got this stupid cough." Danny blew his nose, then said, "Besides, if Mr. Parker went to southern Missouri, near the Kansas border, it was more than a day's ride. He had to spend the night somewhere and get a doctor's help for his arm."

"Maybe Mrs. Parker didn't tell enough in her letter. That's not Miss Hennessey's fault."

"It's the same story that was given out to the neighbors. You're just making excuses for her, Peg." Danny reached for a clean handkerchief and again blew his nose.

"And you—you're lying here in bed with nothing to do but make up ridiculous stories! I know Miss Hennessey better than you do, and she—"

Peg stopped abruptly, as the picture of James, Miss Hennessey's cousin, rose vividly into her mind.

"She what?" Danny asked.

Peg stammered out the story about James, then burst into tears. "But she tried to convince him he's wrong," she sobbed. "Miss Hennessey is loyal to the Union. She told me she is!"

By the time Peg had pulled herself together, wiping her eyes on the corner of Danny's bedspread because a handkerchief of her own wasn't handy, she was startled to see that Danny had tossed his nightshirt and mustard plaster on the floor and was fully dressed.

"You're not supposed to get out of bed," Peg protested.

"I told you, I'm all right," Danny said. "Get your coat."

"Where are we going?"

"To visit the Parkers."

"You think they're spies, don't you? Well, they're not!" Peg shot back.

"I didn't say they were spies."

"Just because Mr. Parker was shot, it doesn't mean he was contacting Quantrill. Danny, you know there are plenty of bushwhackers who've robbed and killed innocent people. I believe Mr. Parker's story about being robbed."

"All of it?"

"Well . . ."

"Peg, think about what you've told me. Haven't you wondered, while Miss Hennessey explained, if she was telling the truth?"

"Yes," Peg admitted. "But her answers made sense. They were believable."

Danny put his hands on Peg's shoulders and looked into her eyes. "They were believable because you wanted to believe, didn't you?"

"She brings me here to visit you, Danny." Peg flung her arms about her brother and clung to him. "I want to come. I miss you."

"I miss you, too, and I'm glad you're here, but we need to find out as much as we can about them."

Peg groaned. "Why?"

"Peg, remember. We're at war. Think what could happen to our country if the Confederates win! Would you like it better if I told Ennie and Alfrid what I suspect?"

"No!" Peg vigorously shook her head. "You can't tell anybody, Danny! You know, from what's been going on in southern Missouri, that the military patrols don't ask questions or look for the truth. If they heard of any suspicion, they'd just arrest them—Miss Hennessey, too."

"Then let's you and me find out the truth."

Peg hung back, scowling, so Danny grabbed her

hand. "We can't," she said. "It's cold outside. You'll get sicker if you go out."

Danny opened the chest beside his bed, scattering the stack of clean handkerchiefs on it, and pulled out a knit cap and scarf. As he tugged the hat over his ears he said, "Now are you satisfied?"

"Ennie won't be."

He whipped the scarf around and around his neck. "Ennie doesn't have to know. She's in the kitchen making sweet potato pies, with Gussie there to lend her a hand."

Exasperated, Peg stomped to the door and threw it open. "All right, Danny!" she said. "I'll get my coat, and I'll go with you to visit the Parkers, because I want to prove to you that you're wrong, wrong, wrong!"

With the softest of footsteps they crept downstairs and left the house through the front door. Circling the house, they made their way to the barn.

"Do you mind riding bareback?" Danny asked.

"No," Peg said. She climbed halfway up the side of the stall and swung her left leg onto Flash's broad back.

Danny put the bridle and reins over Flash's head, while Peg leaned down to stroke his neck.

"He's older and quieter," she said, remembering how smartly Flash and Fury had once stepped out as they pulled the Swensons' buggy.

"Maybe he's been lonely since Fury died," Danny said. He opened the stall door, and reins in hand climbed onto the horse in front of Peg. "Hang on to me," he said.

Peg wrapped her arms around his waist and relaxed, adjusting to Flash's rolling movements.

They were quiet as they rode away from the Swensons' house, expecting Ennie to rush outside at any moment, demanding to know where they were off to and what Danny thought he was doing out in this chill air. But no one had noticed them, and soon they were on River Road, taking the turn to the Parkers' house.

The closer they came, the more apprehensive Peg grew. "I think this was a terrible idea!" she complained. "I don't know what to say or what to do."

"Stop worrying," Danny said. "We just decided to pay a call to see how Mr. Parker is faring. It's as simple as that."

"After they tell you how he was shot, will you believe them?"

"I don't know," Danny said. "I hope so."

When they arrived at the Parkers' house a large, mottled gray horse was tied to the hitching post.

"They've got company," Peg said. "Maybe we'd better not go in."

"They'll have already heard or seen us," Danny answered. He jumped off Flash and tied him to the post, then reached up to help Peg down. "I wonder if it's the man I saw riding with Mr. Parker."

"Was he a neighbor? Did you recognize him?"

"No, he wasn't from around here. I've never seen him before."

"Do you remember what he looked like?"

"Yes. No beard or mustache, and long—"

"Good morning."

Peg looked up to see Mrs. Parker in the open doorway, a warm smile on her face.

"Good morning, ma'am," Danny quickly said. "We came to see how Mr. Parker is doing."

"He's recovering nicely," Mrs. Parker said. She glanced over her shoulder into the parlor before she asked, "Won't you come in? How about tea and a muffin or two?"

"Thank you," Peg said, hoping she didn't look as guilty as she felt. She trotted up the steps to the front porch and submitted to Mrs. Parker's energetic hug, but Danny edged around Mrs. Parker at a safe distance as he entered the house.

Mrs. Parker led them past the parlor, which was empty, except for the furniture the Millers had left behind. "Come into the kitchen. It's warmer, and you'll find Violet there."

Peg thought she heard the back door close as they approached, but Miss Hennessey sat alone at the worn wooden table, gazing at them over her teacup, as though nothing could possibly disrupt her quiet, lazy morning.

"They came to ask about Louis," Mrs. Parker said. "Isn't that thoughtful?"

Miss Hennessey beamed affectionately at Peg, then turned her smile on Danny. "Sit down, please," she said. "Nellie has baked the most delicious muffins."

Neither Peg nor Danny had to be asked twice. The muffins were delicious, although Peg nearly choked on hers as Danny bluntly asked, "May we see Mr. Parker?"

"He'll be joining us soon," Miss Hennessey said. "He's recovering nicely and the fever is completely gone."

"I'm glad," Peg said. "You were so sad and so worried about him."

"Worried about me?" Mr. Parker came into the room and sat at the table with the others. He wore a loose, collarless shirt that fit snugly over the bulge of a bandage around his upper right arm. "There was no need to worry. I come from hardy stock." He smiled at

108

Danny. "You must be Miss Kelly's brother. I've heard many fine things about you."

Danny automatically reached out a hand, and looked embarrassed when Mr. Parker extended his left hand, instead of his right. "I'm sorry you were shot," Danny said.

Peg winced as he added, "Peg didn't know the whole story of what happened to you, and if you don't mind, sir, I'd like to hear it, too."

"There's not much to tell," Mr. Parker answered. "I had ridden south to Butler and had planned to go even farther to see someone about purchasing some livestock."

"That's quite a ways to go for livestock," Danny interrupted.

"The owner's a friend. He offered me a good price."

Livestock? Peg wondered. *When their stay here is supposed to be a temporary one?*

Mr. Parker went on as though Danny's statement was of no importance, but Peg could sense a tension in the room. Both Mrs. Parker and Miss Hennessey were listening intently.

"I had no warning. I was riding through some pretty desolate countryside when I heard the crack of a rifle, and the bullet slammed into my arm."

"Who shot you? Did you see them?"

"It was just one man. I was so startled I took time to turn to look, and there he was, riding toward me from a grove of trees."

"Oh!" Peg cried and squeezed her fingers together, vividly imagining the pain and the fear that Mr. Parker must have known.

"My horse is both sturdy and fast so, fortunately, I was able to outrun my attacker. I found help at a farm near Butler, and after my wound was cleaned and bandaged I rode on home."

"Alone?"

"Alone."

From the corners of her eyes Peg saw Danny turn to look at her, but she refused to meet his glance.

Mr. Parker looked from Danny to Peg, then added, "As I said, I was alone, except that as I approached River Road I met an acquaintance who saw the plight I was in and accompanied me to the house."

This time Peg, with a flash of triumph, did meet Danny's eyes. That certainly explained what he had seen, and should have ended his suspicions once and for all.

But Danny didn't give up. "Weren't you afraid of running into Quantrill?" he asked. "He and his raiders were in those parts."

Mrs. Parker broke in. "Everyone's afraid of Quantrill."

Peg was startled at the deep sorrow in her eyes. It was a mirror of Miss Hennessey's expression, and she was puzzled. Here was Louis Parker, safe and sound, with his wound healing well. Shouldn't that make them happy?

Mrs. Parker got to her feet. "I'm going to wrap up some of these muffins for you to take to Mrs. Swenson," she said. "Louis needs to rest, although I know he enjoyed your visit. We all did."

She left no doubt they were being dismissed, so Peg and Danny rose, too, accepted the muffins with thanks, and wished Mr. Parker a complete and successful recovery.

As they climbed on Flash's back, Peg couldn't resist whispering, "Mr. Parker *was* telling the truth! See how wrong you were?"

"I see things you don't see," Danny retorted.

"Like what?"

He waited until they had left the Parkers' house behind and were back on River Road before he answered. "Like the horse."

"What horse?"

"The horse that was tied to the hitching post when we arrived."

"Oh," Peg said, surprised. "I forgot about the horse."

"Didn't you hear the back door close before we entered the kitchen? Someone left the house in a hurry when we arrived—someone who didn't want us to know he was there."

Peg took a deep breath. She could hear the determination in her voice as she said, "Then we haven't a choice. Somehow we'll need to find out who he was and why he was there."

12

JUST AS PEG had expected, Ennie was greatly displeased about Danny's escape from his bed and from his mustard plaster. She quickly stirred together a mixture for a new poultice, wrapped it in cheesecloth, and pinned it to a clean nightshirt, warning him of dire consequences if he were to leave his bed again without permission.

"But we wanted to give Mr. Parker our regards," Danny said, then tried to smother a cough.

"I've already done that," Ennie informed him, "and brought the poor man some soup, besides."

Does everyone send soup to sick people? Peg wondered. *Does it really make them feel better?*

"We even brought you some of Mrs. Parker's muffins," Danny said.

"I can do without the muffins, thank you," Ennie

told him. "They're a little heavy, but then Mrs. Parker doesn't have my light hand with batter nor my special receipt."

Danny gave in. "I'm sorry I disobeyed you," he said.

"And well you might be," Ennie told him. She placed a hand on his forehead. "You seem a mite feverish. I'll give you a dose of tonic."

"Not tonic, please! It's nasty-tasting stuff!"

Danny grimaced as Ennie poured a dark, clear liquid into a large spoon and held it out, making sure Danny swallowed every drop. Peg tried not to giggle at the miserable faces he was making. She had warned Danny that Ennie would be upset, and she'd been right.

Ennie kept a sharp eye on both Danny and Peg, but she did allow Peg to play draughts with Danny, read to him, and carry up countless cups of a honey and lemon juice mixture, thinned with strong tea.

She hovered so closely that Danny was unable to say any more to Peg about the Parkers until it was almost time for Peg to leave.

"Find out what you can about who that was in the Parkers' house," he whispered.

Peg sighed, wishing her visits to Danny could be uncomplicated, with no stupid suspicions to worry about. "Most likely, he was just a neighbor stopping by," she said.

"Ask."

"What if Miss Hennessey won't tell me?"

"Then find out some other way."

"How?"

Exasperated, Danny grumbled, "Stop acting so stubborn. You can be a snoop when you want to be, so figure out a plan yourself. In the meantime I'll keep an eye on the Parkers' house."

"Ennie won't let you. She'll make you stay in bed until you're better."

"Never fear, I'll be better soon. You and I, Peg—we'll do what we can to help our country win this war."

Frantic with the hopelessness of the task, Peg snapped, "Winning the war is a job for generals. You're only thirteen, and I'm eleven. How much can we do to help the Union?"

"Whatever we can. We're Kellys," he said, "and Kellys don't give up. Think of Mike and what he tried to do."

"Miss Hennessey is my friend," she complained. "I can't believe she's doing something to hurt the Union."

"Then prove me wrong."

"All right, Danny Kelly! You'll see! I will!"

"And don't look so scared," he called as she left his room. "You'll give yourself away."

"Oh, shut up, Danny! I am not scared!"

But she was. She was terrified of what she might find out. Peg tried to push away the questions she'd had about Miss Hennessey, but they wouldn't leave and kept darting into her thoughts like biting, stinging insects.

As Peg reluctantly dragged down the stairs, her carpetbag bumping against her legs, she thought of Mike's and Frances Mary's bravery, which Miss Hennessey had pointed out. And she thought about Megan—shy, quiet Megan—who had fought off wolves and an armed robber in order to protect her family.

And Danny, himself, who had stood up against bushwhackers who had tried to destroy the farm and take his life.

I want to be brave like Frances and Megan and Mike and Danny, Peg told herself. *Frances was*

*scared. She told us so. And Megan, too. But they did
what they had to do, and I can, too.*

Determined, she clumped down the last two stairs,
hugged Ennie and Alfrid, and ran outside to climb into
Miss Hennessey's buggy.

As they reached the road that would take them
home, Peg sat up as straight as she could and said,
"I'm glad that Mr. Parker is feeling better."

"Thank you," Miss Hennessey said.

"I hope you didn't mind that Danny and I paid your
family a visit."

"On the contrary. You were very gracious to do so."

Peg realized she was fidgeting and clasped her
hands tightly together. "Did we come when we
shouldn't have? I guess we surprised you."

Miss Hennessey quickly turned toward Peg. "Why
do you say that?"

Peg took a deep, shaky breath. "Because someone
was at the house. He left when we got there."

"Oh? What makes you think so?"

"There was a gray spotted horse tied to the hitching post when Danny and I rode up. When we came
back outside the horse was gone."

For a moment Miss Hennessey was silent. Then she
said, "As I recall, one of Louis's neighbors had come
by to talk to him."

"You didn't see the neighbor?"

Miss Hennessey's eyes bore into Peg's. "Did you?"

Peg shook her head, wondering what to ask next.

Miss Hennessey quietly asked, "Does it really matter, Peg?"

"I don't know," Peg answered truthfully. How far
could she go in what she told Miss Hennessey? Maybe
there was a better way to find out about the Parkers'

visitor. She'd give it more thought and not continue blundering along with questions that led nowhere.

Peg glanced down a nearby hill, aware that the luster of the red-gold leaves was fading. Shivering even though her coat was warm, she said, "Winter is coming quickly. There's a real chill in the air."

"There is indeed," Miss Hennessey answered. She began to talk about the heavy snows of the previous winter and how they caused such terrible problems to soldiers in the field, who often were lacking protective clothing, such as shoes and coats.

Although Peg was frustrated that Miss Hennessey hadn't given her straightforward answers, she felt a tiny glimmer of relief that she didn't have to face problems too large right now to handle. *Please, please, please!* Peg agonized. *What will I do if Miss Hennessey and her relatives are Confederate spies!*

The ride home was uneventful, with not even a Union patrol in sight. But when Peg and Miss Hennessey arrived in St. Joseph they discovered that all that was left of the town's newspaper building was blackened rubble and the stench of burnt, wet wood.

Miss Hennessey leaned from the buggy to ask a man standing nearby, "What happened?"

The man pulled off his cap and looked both ways before he answered. "This is all on account of Colonel John Williams."

"The Commander of the St. Joseph Military District?"

"That's him. He didn't like some of the articles in the *Gazette*. Said they were inflammatory. So he sent a military squad to talk to the editor, and a mob formed and followed along. When the editor saw them coming, he jumped on his horse and got the sam hill out of here. Just in time, because the mob destroyed the presses and burned down the building."

Miss Hennessey flicked the reins, urging the horse on, until they arrived at Peg's house.

Peg thought of John enjoying every word in his newspaper. Now St. Joseph didn't have a newspaper. "Why did they do that?" she mourned.

Although Peg didn't expect an answer, Miss Hennessey said, "It's true that the editor wrote some inflammatory articles about the military control of Missouri."

"But he wasn't a southern sympathizer!"

"Let's get inside," Miss Hennessey said. "It's growing colder by the minute."

Ma was full of questions, but the talk kept bouncing from Danny's welfare and the state of Louis Parker's health to the carnage of *The St. Joseph Gazette.*

John had much to say about that. "Old J.H.R. Cundiff wrote his articles the way he saw them. He was right about the unfairness of the military police in Missouri. The heavy-handed actions of a few men in power have actually driven loyal supporters over to the Confederate side."

Finally, the conversation ebbed. Miss Hennessey left to return the buggy, with the promise she'd see them soon, and John strode into the backyard to carry in a load of wood.

"At last we can talk!" Ma said. She grasped Peg's shoulders and smiled. "Tell me about Danny."

"There's nothing to tell," Peg said, surprised. "He's fine. That is, except for a sniffle and a cough."

"A sniffle and cough?"

"Ennie put him in bed with a mustard plaster on his

117

chest, but we played draughts and I read some to him."

"If he'd been put to bed, it must have been more than you're saying," Ma told her.

"Danny's nose was red, but he told me he felt fine," Peg answered.

"Then I suppose there's nothing to worry about," Ma said, but Peg heard the concern still in her voice. "I'm sure Ennie is taking good care of my boy."

Peg saw no reason to worry Ma by telling her that Danny had got out of bed—against orders—and had gone out in the chill air to visit the Parkers, because then she'd have to say *why* Danny wanted to investigate the Parkers; and that would bring in Miss Hennessey, and there was nothing to be held against Miss Hennessey except a few suspicions. Peg didn't doubt for a minute that if Ma became aware of even one small suspicion, the trips to visit Danny would come to a quick end.

Peg sighed and said, "I'm hungry."

Ma smiled. "There are apples in the cooler, love. Eating one now won't spoil your supper." She paused. "I suppose that Ennie Swenson cooked some fine dishes for you to enjoy."

Peg shrugged. "They were all right, Ma, but your cooking's a lot better."

"Is it now?" Ma said, the pleasure in her voice as warm and soft as butter.

She bustled off to the kitchen, leaving Peg to wonder: What should she do next to discover the identity of the Parkers' visitor? She wished she could ask Frances Mary for advice. If she and her big sister could change places, what would Frances do?

*   *   *

Except for those who grumbled now and then about missing *The St. Joseph Gazette*, the excitement over the fire soon died down and the residents of the town once again were caught up in their busy existence.

Peg, who was unwilling to talk to even her best friends about her trips with Miss Hennessey, bent all her energies toward her studies, winning Miss Thomas's praise.

But Marcus wouldn't let Peg be. One day at lunchtime he sneaked around behind the bench on which Peg was sitting with May and April, caught a fistful of her hair, and pulled hard.

"Ouch!" Peg yelled. She jumped up to run after Marcus, but he was already out of reach, hiding behind Willie, leaning out only to stick out his tongue.

"I hope your face freezes like that, Marcus Hurd!"

"Maybe it will, and you and I could be the ugly stepsisters in the Cinderella story Miss Thomas read us."

"Huh! What could a guttersnipe like you know about Cinderella?"

"I know this much—that even when you're high and mighty riding in a buggy and thinkin' you're Cinderella yourself, you're not!" Marcus bent double with laughter, and Willie joined in.

"They're both very common," May said loftily. "Ignore them, Peg."

April tugged at Peg's skirt until Peg plopped back down on the bench. "Marcus likes you," April whispered.

Peg's eyes flashed angrily. "He's horrid! He's ugly-squished-dead-bug horrid!"

April shrugged and bit into a thick roll of bread and cheese. "He still likes you."

Marcus dared to creep a little closer. "Someday I'll rent a fine buggy, too, and maybe you'll want to go riding with me, and maybe I won't ask you."

"Good," Peg said. "Don't ask me."

"Maybe you'll want to hold my lucky arrowhead, and I won't let you."

"I'm not interested in your stupid lucky arrowhead!" Peg bit into an apple with a loud crack, the tart juice running down her throat and making her shiver.

Marcus began to prance around and flutter his hands. In a falsetto voice he said, "Oh, Peg, I must tell you an amusing story about one of Mrs. Kling's boarders!" . . . "A wonderful story, Miss Hennessey" . . . "Peg, my dear girl . . ."

In shock, Peg leaped to her feet. "You slimy snake! You spied on us!"

"Of course I did. How else would I find out what you were talking about?" Marcus hooted, and Willie snickered, both of them dancing out of Peg's reach.

" 'Peg's mad, and I'm glad, and I know what will please her. A bottle of ink to make her stink and Marcus Hurd to tease her!' " Willie chanted.

But Peg had stopped listening, her mind dwelling on what Marcus had said. He had spied because it was the only way to find out what she and Miss Hennessey had been talking about. And she had promised Danny to spy, too. Sinking slowly to the bench, ignoring the lunch Ma had packed for her to eat, Peg moaned, and May quickly turned to her. "Are you sick?" she asked.

"No," Peg said, shaking her head, but she *was* sick. Sick at the idea of subterfuge. *I'll give Miss Hennessey one more chance to answer my questions*, Peg told herself, *before I even begin to think of other ways to find out the information Danny wants. I'll go to Mrs. Kling's boardinghouse the minute school is over and talk to Miss Hennessey. I know she'll be truthful with me. I know she's not a Rebel spy! She can't be!*

At exactly four o'clock Miss Thomas gave her students their assignments for the next day and marched them to the door in neat lines. Not even waiting to walk home with May and April, Peg broke free and ran down the hill, hair flying and skirts flapping.

She burst into the door, dropped her books on the kitchen table, and yelled, "Ma? Where are you?"

From upstairs Ma answered, "Here I am, love."

"I'm going out for a little while, Ma!" Peg shouted. "I'll be right back."

Not wanting to hear Ma's answer, Peg slammed the door and ran outside, heading down the hill into town. She wove through the busy street traffic, but when she came to the block on which Mrs. Kling's boardinghouse was located, she hesitated. She couldn't just march up and knock at the door and ask to see Miss Hennessey without a plan in her head. What would be her reason for coming? What excuse could she devise?

In order to give herself time to think, Peg skirted the block, her mind whirling with ideas that wouldn't come together and make sense. So desperate was Peg to come up with the right things to say, she stopped watching where she was stepping and tripped over a small pile of rubbish at the entrance to an alley. Down she fell, the rough stones stinging her knees as they cut through her black cotton stockings.

Tugging an almost-clean handkerchief from her coat pocket, Peg scrunched down behind some piles of boxes and rubbed the dirt from her knees. Ma would have a fit about the stockings, which was bad enough, but now Peg couldn't visit Miss Hennessey—not with stockings torn and bloody.

Boot heels suddenly slapped the cobblestones so

close to where Peg was huddled that she flinched and pressed back against the boxes. A tall man strode past —a beardless man with long hair and . . .

Peg gasped. In a homespun shirt and trousers he was dressed differently from when Peg had first seen him, but she knew him immediately. James! Miss Hennessey's renegade cousin!

13

PEG SLOWLY CLIMBED to her feet. If James had gone with Quantrill's raiders, then by now he should be in Arkansas, on his way to Texas. What was he doing here, dressed in farmer's homespun with a broad-brimmed felt hat pulled low over his eyes?

Danny's partial description of the man he'd seen riding with Mr. Parker flashed into Peg's mind. *No beard or mustache and long . . . Had Danny been about to say long, curly hair?*

Danny!

Peg suddenly woke up to the fact that she was shivering in the alley when she could be following James, as Danny would want her to do. James's big boots had carried him well into the alley, so Peg took that route, too, this time quietly and carefully picking her way over and around the rubble, much of it hidden by the late afternoon's deep shadows.

She was close to the next street when she heard a voice. She looked up and saw that James was still inside the alley, nearly hidden in the dim light. And with him was a woman.

Her heart pounding, her throat tight with fear and hurt, Peg huddled against the wall. Although she couldn't see the woman clearly, Peg knew that she had to be Miss Hennessey. Who else would James meet so secretly? And if this was Miss Hennessey, then everything she had told Peg was a lie! And Peg had believed it!

Peg's heartache slid into anger, and she stepped out boldly, ready to confront Miss Hennessey. But the couple had left, and the alley was empty.

Bloody, torn stockings or not, Peg marched furiously out into the street and down the block to Mrs. Kling's boardinghouse.

"Please, may I see Miss Hennessey?" Peg asked Mrs. Kling as she opened the door.

"Why, you're the little girl who visited her before," Mrs. Kling said and held the door open wide. But she took in Peg's appearance immediately, and her smile changed to a look of concern. "Whatever in the world happened to you?" she asked, automatically bending down to brush dirt from Peg's coat.

"I fell on the cobblestones," Peg answered.

"My, my, my! Will you look at those knees! You're in need of some cool water and a cloth to clean those scrapes."

"Maybe Miss Hennessey . . . ," Peg began, but Mrs. Kling was already leading Peg up the stairs and down the hall to the third room on the right.

Mrs. Kling knocked on the door, waited for an answer, then knocked again. "Apparently, Miss Hennessey is not at home," she said. "If you'd like, you may wait for her in the parlor."

Peg tugged at her skirts, her face pink with embarrassment at the thought of her skinned knees on exhibit for anyone who came into the parlor. "Please, ma'am, the state my stockings are in . . . Could I wait in Miss Hennessey's room, instead?"

From her pocket Mrs. Kling pulled a round gold watch on a chain, glanced at it and said, "Supper will be served in fifteen minutes, so Miss Hennessey should arrive home any minute now. I suppose that under the circumstances, there's nothing wrong with allowing you to wait in her room." She opened the door, sailed inside with a swish of skirts, and lit the oil lamp on the nearest table. "Sit down, dear," she said, "and do tend to those knees as soon as possible."

Out the door Mrs. Kling swept, closing it firmly behind her.

Peg studied the room. It was neat and tidy, with lacy curtains and two floral prints on the wall. A puffy patchwork quilt covered the bed, and a wardrobe stood against the far wall.

Unable to resist temptation, Peg opened both wardrobe doors wide and peered inside. There hung the dull gray dress Miss Hennessey had worn while she stayed at their house, and the traveling suit she had worn to visit her sister, but there were two beautiful dresses in velvet and silk hanging next to them. Peg stroked the soft fabric and wondered where Miss Hennessey could possibly wear such elegant dresses.

The two carpetbags were against the wall behind the wardrobe. Peg quickly closed the wardrobe doors and opened the bags. The small one was completely empty, the clothing inside probably transferred to the chest of drawers; but the bottom of the larger one contained printed leaflets.

Peg picked one up and saw that it advertised a play that had been performed at a theater in St. Louis. Another was from a theater in New York. On both leaflets was a sketch of a beautiful, dark-haired woman who could be no one else but Miss Hennessey. But the printed name of the actress under the picture was Elsie Morgan.

Stunned, shaken, and unable to comprehend what she had discovered, Peg staggered to the edge of the bed and plopped down. Who was Elsie Morgan? Who was Violet Hennessey? Ma would have a fit if she knew Miss Hennessey was an actress. And surely Mrs. Kling didn't know, either. No respectable landlady of a boardinghouse would rent a room to an actress. Actresses were . . . well . . . Peg wasn't exactly sure why actresses were shunned by other women, but she remembered the painted ladies she'd seen in the hotel when she and Danny were there with Olga and Alfrid, and she'd heard comments about actresses being "loose women," whatever a loose woman was.

As the door suddenly opened behind her Peg started with fright and jumped to her feet. For just an instant Miss Hennessey stared at Peg with wide eyes. Then she silently closed the door and crossed the room. She took the leaflets from Peg's hands, returned them to the carpetbag, and snapped it shut.

Although she was frightened, Peg asked, "Who are you?"

"As you've discovered," Miss Hennessey said, "I'm an actress."

"But are you Violet Hennessey or Elsie Morgan?"

"Does it matter?"

"Yes. Of course it matters."

"Why? Do you like me any the less because you've learned about my profession?"

Peg's cheeks grew warm as anger flooded her body. "I don't have to explain," she insisted. "*You* do!"

Miss Hennessey removed her coat and hat and sat on a small, slat-backed rocker. Calmly, she said, "Are you aware that most people look down their well-bred noses at actresses? It's a popular conception that we are not as moral as other women."

Peg nodded, still not quite sure what Miss Hennessey meant.

"I hope you won't inform your mother or Mrs. Kling about my profession. I hope that for a little while this can be our secret, Peg."

"Our secret!" Peg exploded. "How many times have you asked me to keep your secrets?"

"I ask only because we're friends."

"If we were friends, we'd tell each other the truth."

"Oh? Do you think we've been untruthful with each other?"

"No! Yes! No! I mean, *I* haven't been the one who has hidden things. But *you* have! You've lied to me! And to Ma! Over and over again!"

Peg dropped to the bed again, her outburst of anger draining her energy.

"If that's what you believe, what can I possibly say that will change the situation?" Miss Hennessey asked. She pulled a handkerchief from her sleeve and dabbed at her eyes.

"You can tell me the truth," Peg said, not for one moment believing that Miss Hennessey's tears were real. "Are you a Confederate spy?" She shivered as the spoken word, *spy*, soured her mouth and slammed against her ears.

"What reason could you possibly have to suspect me of such treason?"

"There you go again!" Peg cried in frustration. "You answer my questions with other questions. You don't give me the answers I want."

"Exactly what is it you want?"

"I told you—I want the truth! I saw you with James in the alley, and I think James is the man who rode home with Mr. Parker after he was injured. Danny thinks Mr. Parker is the one who told Quantrill that the Union general's wagon train was coming, so Quantrill could attack it." She took a long breath that ended in a sob, as she said, "Danny wanted to tell the Union authorities, but I begged him not to. I told him you were my friend, and I believed in you. But I don't anymore. Now I wish I'd told him to go ahead and tell."

"I've hurt you," Miss Hennessey said. "I truly didn't mean to hurt you." She held out a hand, but Peg refused to take it.

Chimes sounded from the foot of the stairs, signaling that supper was about to be served. Peg stood, ready to leave, but Miss Hennessey waved her back. "Please stay," she said. "Supper isn't important, Peg. *You're* important. I'll answer your questions . . . truthfully. I promise."

Slowly Peg sat down, even though she seriously doubted Miss Hennessey's promises and truthfulness.

"However, I must ask you, in return," Miss Hennessey said, "not to reveal what I'm about to tell you."

"I can't promise that," Peg said, "when I don't know what you're going to say. I'm tired of lies and secrets. And I can't hide information that would aid the enemy and hurt the Union."

Miss Hennessey thought for a long moment, then said, "I understand, and you're right to feel the way you do. I'll tell you what I can, and then you'll know why the information must be kept secret."

"Fair enough," Peg answered. She folded her arms tightly across her chest and prepared to listen.

"Give me a moment, please," Miss Hennessey said. She splashed cold water on her eyes, patted her face dry with the linen towel that hung next to the washbasin and pitcher, and went downstairs to inform Mrs. Kling that she would not be having supper.

When she returned she again sat in the rocker. "My stage name is Elsie Morgan," she said. "My true name is Violet Morgan Hennessey. Nellie and Louis Parker are my sister and brother-in-law, but James is not my cousin."

"James is one of Quantrill's raiders!"

"He rode with Quantrill. For a while."

"He's a Confederate."

"Let's not talk of James right now. Let me explain something about myself. I *am* a spy, but not a Confederate spy. I work with a respected Union officer in collecting information that will help our Union Army."

"Is the officer here in St. Joseph?"

"No, but he's within traveling distance."

"Why do you have to travel? Why can't you give the information to one of the officers in St. Joseph?"

"If my work is to be effective, only one man must know who I am. I must be able to trust him, and he must be able to trust me. The Union officers in St. Joseph don't know me, and must not know about me. If my identity were well known, the Confederates would soon learn of it, too, and then my work would be useless."

Peg was insistent. "James was with Quantrill."

Miss Hennessey closed her eyes as though she were exhausted. When she opened them she said, "I learned from James the route Quantrill and his men would take on their ride into Texas. And I later learned about General Blunt's move from Fort Scott to Fort Gibson. I realized the danger Blunt and his company could be in if they crossed paths with Quantrill.

"It would take time to get the information to General Blunt, and I was frantic. I knew I'd be meeting up with Union Army patrols, and I couldn't afford to be stopped and questioned. It was chance that I met your sister, Frances. However, when I learned from her where your brother Danny lived, I knew that the area would be ideal for Nellie and Louis. You'd want the opportunity to see Danny, and if I had a child riding with me my trip likely would not be questioned."

As Miss Hennessey paused, Peg squeezed her eyes shut in agony. "You planned all this before we even met. I thought you invited me to travel with you because you wanted my company."

"I *did* enjoy your company, Peg."

Hurting, Peg hugged her shoulders. "I was just somebody to be there to make things easier for you. You didn't care how you used me."

"I cared about *you*, Peg! Believe me! But I also cared about saving the lives of hundreds of men. That had to come first."

Peg tried to gulp down the lump that tightened her throat. "When you went into the Parkers' house, and I was kept outside, you gave the message to Mr. Parker, didn't you?"

"Yes. Louis was to carry it to General Blunt. But Louis was shot by a bushwhacker who tried to kill and rob him. He didn't get to General Blunt."

"Then that's why you were so sad, wasn't it?"

"Yes. It was terrible to think we had failed."

Peg thought again about that first meeting with the

Parkers. "You only pretended that you hadn't seen your sister for five years, didn't you?"

"That's correct. Nellie and I have worked together for the Union since my husband, Daniel Hennessey, was killed during the first year of the war. Women spies are not shot or hanged when they're caught, so Nellie and I made the decision to work together to help our Union forces."

"What about Mr. Parker?"

"Louis is very brave. He had been wounded in battle and sent home. When he recovered he insisted on joining Nellie and me."

Peg couldn't resist asking, "What might happen to you if someday you're caught?"

Miss Hennessey sighed as she said, "I *was* captured once—in Arkansas—and imprisoned by the Confederates, but my jail was a poorly constructed frame building, and I was able to loosen some boards and escape. I made my way to Kansas, and was almost caught again in the Lawrence massacre."

"Oh!" Peg gasped as the thought struck her. "Frances brought you to our house. Does she know?"

"No," Miss Hennessey answered. "You're the only one in whom I've confided."

She stood and walked to the window, holding aside the lace curtain so she could look out at the streets. For a few minutes neither she nor Peg spoke. Finally, Miss Hennessey turned back to Peg, letting the curtain drop behind her. "I'll leave St. Joseph within a short time. I'll make contact with my Union officer and give him the extremely important information I was sent here to learn."

"Did James give you that information?"

"There's no need for you to know my source," she answered.

As Peg tried to sort out all that she'd heard, Miss Hennessey said, "You can see that my life—and Nellie's and Louis's lives—are in your hands."

"Don't say that!" Peg insisted. "It isn't fair!"

Miss Hennessey's eyes were deep and dark, her gaze intent on Peg's face. "Fair? It's hard to think about being fair. I have answered your questions truthfully, and I promise that I'll never ask you to travel with me again. As I told you, soon I'll leave St. Joseph, probably never to return."

Her mind in a torment, Peg studied Miss Hennessey. Like the little chameleon lizard Marcus had once caught and brought to school—its skin changing from brown to green and brown again—Miss Hennessey now was neither the beautiful, self-assured woman nor the timid, mousy woman Peg had known. She looked tired and frail and so pitiful that, in spite of her quandary, Peg's heart ached for her.

"Will you keep my secret? What is your answer, Peg?" Miss Hennessey asked.

Peg couldn't speak. She needed time to think. What *could* she answer?

14

When Peg dragged through the back door, Ma was in what Mr. Murphy called "a real stew."

"Where have you been so late?" Ma demanded.

Peg's only answer was to hold her skirts up over her knees.

Ma took a look at Peg's legs, pushed her into the nearest kitchen chair, and bent to examine her knees more closely. "Merciful heavens!" she said. "Pull off those stockings, missy, and we'll tend to cleaning the scrapes. How in the world did you do this?"

"I fell," Peg said.

"Chasing that Marcus Hurd, no doubt. I have a good mind to speak to the boy's mother, although from what I hear she has plenty of other family problems to contend with."

As Ma went on, her steam slowly dying down like

the steam from a kettle taken from the fire, Peg held her tongue. For now her mind was filled with what Miss Hennessey had told her and what she had answered.

She had believed Miss Hennessey. She had to believe. "I'll keep your secret," Peg had told her, even though the responsibility of the promise had scared her right down to her toes.

"Ouch!" she muttered as Ma pried a tiny pebble from the torn skin.

"Sorry, love," Ma said. "I'm trying to be as gentle as possible, but I have to get all the dirt out." She sighed. "You want me to think of you as grown up, and then you come home with a perfectly good pair of stockings torn to shreds, and looking as disheveled as though you'd been in a fight. That Marcus!"

"Don't blame Marcus," Peg said. "It wasn't his fault."

"So you're the one who started it this time, are you?"

"I don't want to talk about it."

"I can't say that I blame you."

"Ma, I'm sorry! Let's not talk about it anymore. Please?"

Silently, Ma sponged and patted, then wrapped Peg's skinned knees in soft, clean cloths. She had no sooner finished than John arrived home.

He hung his coat on a peg near the back door and turned to his wife, sadly shaking his head. "Even though I'm Federal and loyal to the bone, I'm thinking that putting the state of Missouri under military rule might have been a big mistake."

"The military had to do something to stop the southern sympathizers," Ma countered. She washed her hands and began to dish up bowls of what looked and smelled like a delicious vegetable stew. "They were threatening Federals, burning their barns and houses, and running them off their land."

"Well, now the sympathizers have been bold enough to slip into St. Joe again. They've done a terrible thing. They recognized a man who they claimed was posing as a Confederate, but whom they suspected of being a Union spy. They chased him down, dragged him out of town before the authorities could act, and hanged him from the branch of an old oak tree near the river."

Peg grew so cold she felt faint, and the spoon she'd been holding dropped from her hand. "Who was the man?" she whispered.

John shrugged. "I don't know. No one from around here, I was told."

Ma sank into her chair, her shoulders drooping. "This terrible war has to end soon," she said, "before we are all destroyed."

Was the murdered man James? Peg wondered. *And if he was, and it's known that he'd brought information to Miss Hennessey, then what will become of her? Will she be arrested and imprisoned, as she said she might?*

"Peg? Peg? Where are you off to, love?"

Peg realized that Ma was speaking to her. "I'm sorry, Ma," she managed to say. "What did you ask me?"

"You're not eating," Ma said. "I asked why."

"I—I don't feel like eating." So cold that she shivered, Peg pressed her hands against the pain in her stomach. "I feel sick, Ma. I hurt."

Noreen pressed a hand against Peg's forehead. "You haven't got a fever. That's a good sign," she said.

"I—it's m-my knees," Peg stammered, desperately searching for an excuse. "I—I just want to go to bed."

"They hurt that much? Well then, upstairs with you, love, and if you need or want anything—a nice soothing cup of peppermint tea, perhaps—just call me."

"Thanks, Ma." Peg scooted from her chair, bent to kiss Ma's forehead, and headed for the stairs.

"What's this about her knees?" she heard John ask, but Peg was in her room before Ma began her explanation.

Snuggled under her warm quilt and ignoring the sting of her skinned knees, Peg tried to sort out her thoughts. Miss Hennessey had said that she now had the information she needed. Although she hadn't admitted that James had brought it to her, he was the one whom she'd met in the alley.

Peg was sure that the Union spy who'd been hanged was James. And she was equally sure that Miss Hennessey would try to leave St. Joe as soon as possible.

She wouldn't travel at night. That would be much too dangerous. But come morning light, she'd probably leave, heading for Nellie and Louis Parker's house on River Road.

Without Peg.

Peg gave a little moan. Miss Hennessey had promised: "I'll never ask you to travel with me again." But she'd be in danger traveling alone. Peg had no idea what information she was bringing the Union officer. Maybe it was a spoken message. But maybe, since the information was so important, it was written down. With a young companion she could seem to be just a mother traveling with a daughter. But if she were alone, she'd be vulnerable to being stopped and searched.

Peg groaned, stuffing the edge of the quilt into her mouth to stifle the sound. *I can't desert her. I can't let her travel alone. What should I do?*

She thought again about Mike, who had gone into battle, risking his life for the Union. She thought about Frances Mary, who had bravely smuggled runaway slaves into Canada. And she thought about Danny, who was so eager to help his country.

Peg had told Danny, "There are other ways to help the Union besides fighting." And here was one of those ways—dropped right into her lap. She could be every bit as brave as her brothers and sisters and ride with Miss Hennessey, helping her to get her important information to the Union Army. All she had to do was plan a way to make it happen.

Tossing and squirming from side to side on sheets that had been pulled out and rumpled, Peg wondered how she could possibly work out a plan. If she explained everything to Ma, she'd have a fit and keep Peg home, safely under her care. So she couldn't tell Ma. Although Peg had hated keeping secrets from Ma, she still had done it; but under no circumstances would she deliberately deceive Ma. What was she going to do?

Exhausted, she finally slipped from bed and quietly opened her bedroom door. The house was dark and quiet, except for the rhythmic rumble of John Murphy's snoring.

Peg gently closed the door, made her way to the small desk in her room, and lit the oil lamp. From a drawer she pulled a sheet of paper. She fitted a penpoint into its holder, and opened a bottle of ink. She'd write to Ma. So very much had happened—enough to fill pages—but she'd tell Ma all the important things, at least. And she'd tell her where she had gone, so early in the morning.

Ma would find the letter when Peg didn't appear downstairs, but by that time Peg was sure that she and Miss Hennessey would be on their way.

Peg bent over the paper, writing quickly, but dipping the pen carefully so drops of ink wouldn't blot her letter. She had written most of what she wanted to say when the door suddenly opened, and there stood Ma, clutching her wrapper together over her flannel nightgown. Startled, Peg dropped the pen.

"What are you doing?" Ma asked.

"I—I'm writing a letter."

"There's something very much the matter, Peg. What is it?"

Peg jumped up from her chair, ran to Ma, and wrapped her arms around her. As Ma hugged her in return, Peg's brave resolutions vanished, and she tucked her face into Ma's shoulder, not even trying to stop her tears.

Holding tightly, Ma guided Peg to the bed, where they sat side by side, Ma gently murmuring, snuggling, and patting, until Peg's tears turned into dry shudders and sobs.

"There now, love," Ma said. "The storm is over. Can we talk about what has upset you so much?"

"Oh, Ma," Peg said. "I wish the war was over."

"As do we all," Ma answered. "Is it the tales John brings home that are frightening you?"

Peg nodded. "That and the awful thing that happened to the spy . . . and . . . all of it."

"Do you want to talk about it?"

"No. I don't. I can't. Not right now."

Here she was, keeping things from Ma again, just what she didn't want to do. But Peg reminded herself

that when Ma read the letter in the morning, everything would be explained. It wasn't as though she were
lying to Ma. She was just delaying in telling her what
had happened and what was going to happen.

"What were you writing?" Ma asked, startling Peg
so much that she jumped.

"A letter," Peg answered.

Ma's arms were firm and strong, and she gave Peg
an extra hug. "I understand," she said. "Sometimes it's
easier to put thoughts down on paper or talk them
over with a sister than with anyone else. Well, if you're
writing to Frances and Megan, give them my love."

Peg didn't try to explain. She didn't even have
enough strength to fight the guilt that crawled up and
down her backbone like one of Marcus's squirmy,
slimy bugs.

"I'll smooth your bed, tuck you in, and turn out the
light," Ma said. "It's best you sleep now and finish your
letter in the morning before going to school."

Peg complied, the dark of the room stealing over
her like an extra, cozy blanket. Drained of all thoughts
and feelings, Peg immediately dropped into sleep.

But she woke early, before it was light, her body
recharged and her mind racing.

It took just a line or two to finish the letter to Ma,
and Peg propped it against her pillow. She dressed,
wincing as she pulled her heavy cotton stockings over
the raw spots on her knees. She pulled on her coat,
tucked a shawl over her head and shoulders, and quietly climbed down the stairs, leaving the house
through the front door.

Peg hurried as fast as she could, picking her way
over holes and puddles and nervously jumping at sudden cricks and snicks in the darkness, until she
reached Mrs. Kling's boardinghouse. The sky was light-

ening into a pearl-edged gray, so Peg recognized the boarder who came out of Mrs. Kling's front door as she approached it.

"Good morning," he said, stopping in front of her. "You're Miss Hennessey's young friend, aren't you?"

"Yes," Peg said. "I came to see her."

"Well, you won't find her here," he volunteered. "She left for the stables a few minutes ago."

"The stables?" Peg felt sick with dread. After all her planning, had she missed her?

The boarder smiled again. "Off to visit her sister, she said. But if you hurry, I'm sure you can catch up."

Heedless of the uneven cobblestones, the rubbish that littered the streets, and the pain in her knees, Peg ran as fast as she could in the direction of the stables. She had to catch up with Miss Hennessey! She had to!

As Peg rounded the corner a horse and buggy clip-clopped toward her, and she saw that Miss Hennessey was holding the reins. Arms waving like windmills, Peg brought the buggy to a stop, then scrambled inside.

Miss Hennessey's eyes were wide with surprise. "What are you doing?"

"I'm going with you," Peg said. She settled herself, pulling her shawl more tightly around her.

"You can't."

Peg shook her head. "The man who was . . . hanged. It was James, wasn't it?"

Miss Hennessey nodded, and for the first time, in the thin early light, Peg saw that her eyes were red and swollen.

"You told me you had important information to give to the Union officer you work with," Peg said. "I'm here to help. We both know that you're less likely to be stopped and questioned if I'm with you."

"I'm not returning to St. Joe," Miss Hennessey said quietly. "You'd have no way to get back."

"I wrote to Ma. I told her only as much as she needed to know, and I told her I'd be making the trip with you. She'll come after me."

As Miss Hennessey hesitated, Peg said, "You can't just stay here. You have to leave quickly. Let's go."

Miss Hennessey gave a flip to the reins, and the horse started up. The day was cold and gray, with no hope of sunshine, and the early winter light seemed to pick and probe at broken bricks, holes in the streets, and boarded-up windows in shops from which owners had fled.

Peg shivered. "Do the bushwhackers who killed James know he had given information to you?"

"If they knew," Miss Hennessey said slowly, "I think they would have come to Mrs. Kling's to get me."

"Yes," Peg said with a sigh of relief. "I think so, too."

But Miss Hennessey turned to face Peg. The fear that tightened the muscles around her mouth and widened her eyes leaped like a spark into Peg's heart, squeezing it with a cold hand.

"On the other hand, they may have been chased off by the Union patrols in and around St. Joe," she whispered. "Do they know about me? I really can't be sure."

15

THEY MET A Union patrol just a short distance from St. Joe—one that had stopped them before. The young corporal nodded in recognition, waving away Miss Hennessey's attempt to show him her letter of safe passage.

"Ma'am," he said, "I doubt that you heard about the hanging last night."

Neither Miss Hennessey nor Peg responded, so he added, "Up here in northern Missouri we've had little problem with bushwhackers for months now, but last night a group of about a half dozen of 'em invaded St. Joe. Unless they rode straight off to the south, they're almost bound to be somewhere in this vicinity."

"I'm on my way to visit my sister," Miss Hennessey said softly.

"Yes, ma'am. Could you tell me again where that might be?"

"She lives on River Road, not too far from here."

He looked at his men, then gave a nod. "We'll ride with you a ways."

"Oh, thank you!" Miss Hennessey said and sighed with relief.

"Our pleasure, ma'am."

Peg didn't dare to turn around as the soldiers guided their horses, with a clatter and jingle, into position behind the buggy; but she whispered to Miss Hennessey, "Those are the soldiers who went through the things Ennie sent Ma, but this time they didn't search. They didn't even ask to look through your carpetbags."

"Because the carpetbags aren't with me. I brought nothing with me."

With effort Peg kept herself from craning her neck to stare into the backseat of the buggy. "That means you're going back to St. Joe?"

"No. It means that later I'll send payment to Mrs. Kling for what remains of my room rent and for the cost of shipping my belongings to me."

"But when she packs she'll find out you're an—" Peg clapped her hands over her mouth.

"An actress? Yes. But I'll have left her with a fine, shocking story to tell. It's a fair exchange."

"Where will you go?" Peg asked.

"You know I can't tell you that."

Peg was silent for a moment. Then she said, "But someday will you write to me and tell me where you are? Someday when the war's over?"

"Yes." Miss Hennessey looked down at Peg and smiled. "When the war's over, I will."

They were close to the turn-off at River Road,

when the corporal let out a loud halloo, waved at Miss Hennessey, and led his men back toward St. Joseph.

"I'll take you to the Swensons' and to Danny," Miss Hennessey said. "This is where we'll say goodbye."

"Until 'someday,' " Peg said.

"Yes. Until 'someday.' " Miss Hennessey pulled the horse to a stop and squeezed Peg's hand. "You *did* help me by coming. I'll never forget your kindness and bravery."

"I wasn't brave," Peg said. "I was awfully scared."

"You were brave," Miss Hennessey said firmly. "Now, hurry in. Ennie spotted us from the window, and I don't have time to talk. I have to reach Nellie and Louis as fast as possible."

Peg jumped from the buggy and watched Miss Hennessey drive back to the road. She could see the turn-off where the buggy disappeared among the trees as though it had never existed.

"Well, I swan!" Ennie cried as she scurried out the door and off the back stoop. "Where's she off to so fast, without even so much as a good morning?"

"She's in a terrible hurry," Peg said.

The indignation in Ennie's eyes was replaced by an open curiosity. "Is it her brother-in-law? The fever hasn't returned, has it? All we've heard around here is that he was well on the way to mending."

Peg shrugged. "Where's Danny?" she asked. "Is he in school?"

"It's where he should be, rightly enough, if it weren't for that cough of his. Land sakes, I've tried everything I know, and it still hangs on, so he's down in bed, and that's where you'll find him." Her attention now on Danny, Ennie led Peg to the house, chatting all the way.

But Peg stopped at the back door, gazing back

toward River Road. Something had moved among the trees. Or had it? She stared, but saw nothing out of the ordinary. She must have imagined it.

Peg ran up the stairs toward Danny's room, but entered her old room first. Her window looked out on River Road, whereas Danny's window view was blocked by a tree. Peg stood motionless, partly hidden by the curtain, her eyes on the road. Within a few minutes she saw a rider come up the road and continue until he was out of sight. But soon after him came another rider—a large, heavyset man—who made the turn toward the Parkers' farmhouse.

Dizzy with fear, Peg leaned against the wall for support. There could be an easy explanation for what she'd seen. The first man had gone past, and maybe the second man was a neighbor who'd come to visit the Parkers. But neither of the men looked familiar to Peg, and she was sure she'd recognize most of the Swensons' neighbors.

Peg couldn't explain it, but something didn't feel right.

"Danny!" Peg whispered. She couldn't handle this alone. She needed Danny.

She raced into his bedroom, stopping short at the foot of his bed. Propped up with goosedown pillows, Danny's eyes shone with hope. "At last!" he said. "Something to do! Read to me, Peg! Will you read—"

He broke off, coughing, and Peg frowned at his sunken cheeks and the dark circles under his eyes. "You look terrible!" she said.

"Oh, thanks," he grumbled. "That's just what I needed. Well? Will you read to me?" He coughed again, holding a hand to his chest as if it hurt.

Why, oh why, did Danny have to be sick at that

moment? Peg flopped down on the end of his bed and shook her head.

"I can't read to you now. There's something I have to do."

"What? Ennie isn't going to need you in the kitchen, is she?"

Peg leaned forward. "Danny," she said, "listen to me! I have so much to tell you."

Peg went through the entire story, from seeing Miss Hennessey meet James in the alley to the bushwhackers' raid on St. Joe and the hanging.

Danny sat upright, his eyes glittering. Whether it was from illness or from the horror of the story she told, Peg couldn't tell.

"James," Danny said. "He must have been the man I saw with Mr. Parker."

"I think so," Peg answered.

"So he was a *Union* spy! Not a Confederate at all, but a spy for our Union Army!" Danny sucked in air between his front teeth in a low whistle. "And your Miss Hennessey—a Union spy, too! Think of that!"

"Danny," Peg said, "after Miss Hennessey left me here I saw two men out on River Road. One went by, but the other made the turn into River Road. I watched from the window in my room."

"Do you think he might have been on his way to the Parkers?"

"I don't know. I just feel strange about it, because there never is much traffic on that road."

Danny threw back the covers and struggled to a sitting position. "What do you want us to do?" he asked. He wavered a bit and hung on to the bedpost for support.

"I want to go and make sure Miss Hennessey and

the Parkers are safe, but *you* can't go with me!" Peg insisted. "Look how sick you are!"

"I'm not that sick." Danny gasped and went into a coughing fit.

When he recovered Peg said, "There's probably nothing wrong, but I have to make sure. By this time Miss Hennessey and the Parkers may have left and are well on their way to meet the Union officer who's expecting the information they're bringing. But, if they're not . . ." She stood up, smoothed down the skirt of her coat, and said, "Do you think Alfrid will mind if I borrow Flash?"

"Peg," Danny said. "Why don't we get Alfrid and maybe a few of the neighbors to go with you?"

"What if the men I saw are bushwhackers? You know what they'd do to Alfrid and the others."

Danny sighed. "What if they're bushwhackers and they discover you snooping around?"

Peg shuddered, for a moment closing her eyes, as though she could blot out the frightening picture that flashed into her mind. "They'd probably chase me away, but I don't think they'd hurt me," she said, "because I'm a . . . a child."

"I can't let you go alone," Danny said.

"You have to. You're sick and wobbly, and I'd have to worry about you instead of seeing if Miss Hennessey is all right." She gave Danny a push, and he flopped back onto the bed. Swinging his legs and feet up, Peg tucked the covers around them. "You really are sick," she teased. "Too sick to fight with me."

Danny looked at Peg with concern. "You'll be right back? Soon?"

Peg nodded. "Don't worry. I'm only doing what Frances or Mike—or *you* would do. I'll just make sure the Parkers and Miss Hennessey are safe or that they've left. Then I'll come back. It won't take long."

Danny squeezed Peg's hand. "You were brave to ride with Miss Hennessey, Peg. You said that fighting wasn't the only way to help our Union, and you were right. You helped Miss Hennessey. If she gets her message through, it will be partly because of you. I wish . . . I wish I could do something to help, too."

Peg leaned over to kiss Danny's forehead, even though she knew he'd scrunch up his eyes and pretend to hate it. But this time, to her surprise, he didn't.

"Be careful, Peg," he said.

"I will," Peg told him.

She crept down the stairs, avoided the kitchen, and made her way to the barn, where Flash was stabled. When she lived with the Swensons Danny had shown her how to put a bridle over a horse, slipping the bit into his mouth, so she quickly did as she remembered and climbed on Flash's back, holding the reins tightly.

With a nagging sense of urgency Peg urged Flash into a trot, clinging with her knees to his sides.

In just a short time she arrived at the Parkers' house and was surprised to see two large dappled horses tied to the hitching post. Were these the horses the men she'd seen had been riding? Peg had been watching the men, not the horses, and she couldn't remember.

Suddenly a tall, heavyset man jumped up beside her and grabbed Flash's reins from her hand.

"Quiet!" he ordered. "Just do what I tell you." He led Flash to the hitching post, fastened the reins, and roughly reached up, jerking Peg from Flash's back.

"Go into the house," he said as he gestured with a large handgun.

Her heart pounding so hard that her chest hurt, Peg

managed to stumble up the steps of the porch and enter the house. In the parlor Miss Hennessey and her sister sat together on the old sofa, their ankles and wrists bound. Both women were in tears.

"What did you do to them?" Peg demanded. She whirled toward the man in anger, hating the smug satisfaction on his face.

"We ain't done nothin' . . . yet." He pushed her toward a narrow, ladderback chair. "Sit down, and stay put."

Peg did as she was told. For a few moments the only sound was the heavy breathing of the man with the gun.

Then a deep voice called from the kitchen, "Sully, you want somethin' to eat?"

"Keep it down, Floyd."

"No one's gonna hear us. Come on. There's some meat and some bread."

Scowling, Sully left the room, and they could hear the rumbling of two voices in the kitchen.

"Where's Mr. Parker?" Peg whispered.

"They took him away," Miss Hennessey answered in a low voice.

"We . . . we heard a shot," Mrs. Parker murmured and burst into tears again.

Tears flooded Peg's eyes, too, and for a while she couldn't speak. But she knew they couldn't just sit still and wait for what might happen. "Are they bushwhackers?"

Miss Hennessey nodded.

"Some of the bushwhackers who hanged James?"

"Yes. They bragged about it."

"How many of them are there?"

"There were five, but three of them left. Those two, who call themselves Sully and Floyd, stayed."

"They seem to be waiting for the others to return," Mrs. Parker whispered. She shot an anxious glance toward the kitchen.

Peg lowered her voice. "What happened to the information you were bringing to your Union officer? Did the bushwhackers get it?"

Miss Hennessey's head shot up, and she shook it in warning. "Shhh!" she said.

Content on that score, Peg turned her thoughts to the problem of Sully and Floyd. What were they going to do? And when? "We have to get out of here," Peg whispered.

"We've begged and pleaded. We've even tried to bargain, but nothing has helped. There's not much we can do." Mrs. Parker held up her bound wrists.

Peg didn't answer. She was busy thinking. It would take too long to untie them. The men might come back at any minute. Finally she pointed toward a door in the hallway that connected the parlor with the kitchen. "Is that the cellar door?"

"Yes," Miss Hennessey said.

"Shhh!" Mrs. Parker hissed. "We can't hide in the cellar. And if somehow we did manage to get down there we'd be trapped."

Peg slid out of her chair and picked it up, carrying it to the cellar door, which she opened wide. With a clatter and crash she threw her chair down the stairs, then flattened herself against the wall, the open door covering her, and screamed as though all the banshees in Ireland were after her.

Floyd and Sully pounded into the hallway.

"She fell!" Miss Hennessey screeched. "The little girl fell down the cellar stairs! Help her!"

Peg heard one of the men start down the top steps. Hoping his partner was right behind him, and she'd catch them both off balance, with all her force she swung the door.

But as the door slammed shut, Floyd jumped out of the way. Cursing loudly and rubbing his left arm, Sully shoved the door open and crowded into the hallway next to Floyd.

"I told you to stay put!" Sully shouted at Peg.

Floyd waved a fist near Sully's face. "What's the matter with you, not tyin' up the young'un?"

"She's only a child. I didn't think that—"

"You didn't think at all."

Sully turned his anger on Peg. "You like the cellar?" he snarled. "Fine. It's a good place for all three of you." He and Floyd looked at each other and laughed. "Might as well have them tucked out of the way," Floyd said with a chuckle, "when we set the house afire!"

16

"THAT'S NOT GOING to happen."

Peg gasped as Danny stepped into the room. He held his rifle shoulder high, sighting along the barrel, as he aimed at Sully.

Floyd, who was at that moment unarmed, frantically looked at his empty hands, but Sully's right hand snaked across his chest to the revolver in his belt.

As he whipped it out, Danny pulled the trigger.

Sully shrieked, dropped his gun, and cradled his injured right hand against his chest.

"It's broke! You done broke my hand!" he yelled.

"Get his gun, Peg," Danny said, and as soon as Peg had snatched it up, he ordered the bushwhackers, "Go down in the cellar. Both of you!"

With two guns pointed in their direction, Sully and Floyd obeyed. Peg slammed the cellar door shut and dragged a heavy chest up against it to secure it. As Danny untied Miss Hennessey and Mrs. Parker, Peg added more furniture to the pile at the door. Sully cursed some more and both he and Floyd beat against the door, but the door didn't budge.

"Does the cellar have a window?" Peg asked Mrs. Parker.

"No. It's little more than a root cellar." Mrs. Parker stood and rubbed her wrists.

"Good," Peg said. "Then they won't be getting out of there for—"

Danny's rifle fell to the floor with a crash, and Danny's knees buckled.

"Help me!" Miss Hennessey cried as she caught him under the arms. "He's heavy!"

"Danny! What's wrong?" Peg shouted in terror. She wrapped her arms around his chest, and Mrs. Parker grasped his feet. Among the three of them they managed to settle Danny on the sofa.

"Danny!" Peg cried again.

Miss Hennessey sat beside Danny and began to briskly rub his hands. "Do you have any smelling salts, Nellie?" she asked. "He's fainted."

"Fainted?" Peg asked, bewildered. "But that's not like Danny. I've never known Danny to faint."

While Mrs. Parker hurried to fetch smelling salts, Miss Hennessey rested a hand on Danny's forehead. "His breathing is shallow and raspy. Has he been ill?"

"Yes," Peg said. "He's had a cough." She remembered the strange glitter in his eyes. "And some fever. That's why I wouldn't let him come with me."

The pungent fumes from the smelling salts brought Danny around in a hurry. He tried to struggle to a sitting position, but Miss Hennessey eased him back down and tucked a pillow under his head. "Lie here until you feel stronger," she said.

The men in the basement beat against the door again, and Peg nervously glanced from the door to Miss Hennessey. "You said there were other bush-whackers in the group. You said they'd be back. You'll have to leave now. You can't take the chance of being here when they return."

Mrs. Parker put her fingers to her mouth. "Louis," she whispered. "I can't go now. I have to find Louis."

"I'm sorry, ma'am," Danny broke in. "I found him. I'm sorry." He fell back and closed his eyes.

Mrs. Parker began to cry, but Miss Hennessey stood, gripping her sister's shoulders. "Peg is right," she said. "We must leave. One of us has to get the information to—"

She broke off and took Peg aside, speaking in a low voice. "If we succeed it could mean a major Union victory. I want you to know the particulars, because you and Danny will have played a strong part in bring-ing about this victory.

"Confederate General Bragg holds the city of Chat-tanooga, Tennessee, under siege, which has caused great damage to our troops and rail shipments. I have secret information that Bragg's right-hand man, James Longstreet, plans to leave Chattanooga and take his own troops to Knoxville. With such a large loss of manpower, the Confederates won't be able to hold Chattanooga. If Union forces attack soon, they can de-feat the Confederates and win the city. I must get this information to my contact, who'll inform General Grant."

"Then hurry!" Peg said. "Take the bushwhackers' horses and go!"

Miss Hennessey hesitated. "What about Danny?"

"I'll get Danny home on Flash." Peg forced herself to sound much more confident than she looked. "See, the color's already returning to his face." She looked at Mrs. Parker. "We'll send a Union patrol here. They'll take care of . . . everything. And we'll see that Mr. Parker has a Christian burial."

Sully and Floyd's sudden pounding on the door set them all in motion. Not caring what was proper, Miss Hennessey and Mrs. Parker climbed astride the bush-whackers' horses and raced down the road.

With Peg's support Danny managed to climb on Flash. He pulled Peg up behind him, but soon his energy gave out, and Peg caught his weight as he sagged against her.

Jabbing her heels into Flash's sides, Peg tried to get the old horse to hurry, but Flash complained about the extra weight by snorting and jerking his head up and down. It was all Peg could do to hang on to Danny and, at the same time, keep a firm grip on Flash's reins.

"Ma's coming, Danny. Ma's coming," Peg said over and over again, wondering if she were trying to comfort Danny or herself; and when she reached the turn-off and saw Ma and John Murphy approaching in a buggy, she cried out in relief.

They immediately took charge. Gratefully, Peg relaxed, feeling the way she did when she was slipping into sleep, with someone else to tuck her in, and smooth her blankets, and murmur softly against her hair. John lifted Danny into the buggy as Peg told what had happened, and Ma cradled Danny with one arm, Peg with the other.

"Drive to the Swensons," John told Ma. "I'll take the children's horse and ride back a ways. We passed that Union patrol just a short time ago."

"But you can't tell them *why* Miss Hennessey and the Parkers were attacked! Please!" Peg insisted.

"It's not up to me to give them any information at all beyond what they can see for themselves. There was a bushwhacker attack, a man lies dead, and two of the bushwhackers are imprisoned in a cellar." He studied Peg. "They may want to talk to you, since you were there."

Peg nodded. "It's all right. I'll know what to say."

John glanced at Danny. "The Union boys may help me find a doctor, if there's one left in these parts."

Peg made room for Danny to stretch across Ma's lap, but she tightly hugged Ma's right arm that held the reins. "I told Danny not to come, Ma. Honest, I did. But if he hadn't come . . . well, he did, and he saved our lives."

"Peg, love," Ma murmured, "it's not your fault that Danny's sick. No one's blaming you."

"I had to make a decision. Maybe I made the wrong one if it's hurt Danny. I don't know. It just seemed so important to try to help."

"My dear girl," Ma said. "Part of being a woman is making decisions and accepting responsibility for them, whether they're right or wrong."

"Right now I don't want to be a woman. I'd rather be a child." Peg shuddered. "Danny'll be all right, won't he, Ma? It's just a cough. That's what Danny said."

"We'll see what the doctor has to tell us."

Ma's voice was calm, but Peg shivered with fear as she glanced up at her face and saw the dark shadows of concern that showed what Ma was really thinking.

Danny was soon dressed in a clean nightshirt and tucked into bed. Peg sat close by in his room while

Ennie bathed his forehead, Ma held his hand, and Alfrid stood by, his face twisted with worry. "I'm not hungry," Peg insisted. "I can't eat. I don't want to leave Danny."

But an army officer, who introduced himself as Captain Rolf Allan, arrived at the Swensons and asked to speak to Peg. Reluctantly, she crept downstairs and sat in an overstuffed parlor chair, facing him.

"Miss Kelly," he said, his voice firm and his eyes drilling into hers. "Suppose you tell me who was in that house and exactly what happened."

"Mr. and Mrs. Parker lived there," Peg answered. "Miss Hennessey often came to visit them, and sometimes took me with her so I could visit my brother Danny. This time, when we were stopped by a Union patrol, the leader told us that bushwhackers had invaded St. Joe yesterday and were probably in the area. After Miss Hennessey dropped me off here I noticed a man on horseback turn down River Road, and I wondered if he was going to the Parker house and why. I guess I was thinking about the bushwhackers, and it worried me."

She took a deep breath and continued. "I told Danny I was going to ride to the Parkers on Flash and see if they were all right. And I did. But a man pulled me off Flash's back and pushed me inside the house."

As she described what took place next, Peg grew colder than she'd ever been in her life. Shivering, she hugged her shoulders. "Then Danny fainted," she said, "and when he came to, I took him home."

"Where were the two women who were there?"

"They helped him. One of them had smelling salts."

"They're not there now."

Peg didn't answer, and he asked, "Do you know where they've gone?"

"No," Peg said. "And I can't even guess. They didn't tell me."

Captain Allan stared, but Peg courageously met his gaze. Finally, he got to his feet and said, "Perhaps I should talk to your brother Danny."

"You can try," Peg said without hesitation, "but he's awfully sick. He may not be able to answer you."

The captain strode up the stairs, Peg on his heels, and stopped just inside the open door to Danny's room.

"Danny is too ill to talk to you, sir," Alfrid said sternly.

"I can see that." For the first time Captain Allan looked unsure of himself.

"I know that Peg has told you all that she could," Alfrid said.

"Yes." The captain took an uncertain step backward. "It's just that there are questions about the occupants of that house, and . . ."

"What's there to question?" Ennie stood and faced him, hands on hips. "Bushwhackers have driven many people from their homes. For a while we were free from the bushwhackers' attacks, but now it seems they've returned." She glanced at the open doorway behind the captain. "Gussie," she said, "will you be so kind as to show Captain Allan out?"

Gussie, who had soundlessly crept upstairs, looked frightened, but she said, "Yes'm," and led the captain from the room.

Peg felt a strange pang of regret that she had to keep things hidden from Captain Allan. He was Union, and he was fighting to keep the states together. He wasn't an enemy. He was a friend. But she had promised to protect Miss Hennessey with her secrecy, and she had to keep her promise.

That evening an army doctor arrived. He was stooped, with thin gray hair, and the knuckles on his hands were gnarled and twisted. "Captain Allan's regards," he said. "I seem to be the only doctor around these parts."

He examined Danny, who opened his eyes to watch what the doctor was doing, but who seemed too weak to protest.

The doctor listened to Danny's chest and back with a tubelike device that was attached to something that poked into his ears.

"What's that?" Peg asked.

"It's called a stethoscope," the doctor said. "It helps me listen to your brother's heart and lungs." He folded the stethoscope and put it into the case he had brought with him.

"Why don't you stay with your brother, little girl?" he said. "I'd like to talk to the adults of the family downstairs."

Peg didn't need to hear what the doctor had to say. She could tell by the hopeless look on his face. Ma, Ennie, and Alfrid, all of them pale and frightened, followed the doctor to the parlor.

Scurrying to Danny's side, Peg huddled on the edge of the bed and took his hand. It was cold and as dry as old paper. "Danny!" she said. "Open your eyes and look at me!"

Danny's eyelids fluttered open, but he looked at Peg with such exhaustion she wanted to cry out in protest.

"Danny, we're all going to take good, good care of you, and you're going to get well and strong again."

Danny kept his eyes on hers while he slowly shook his head.

"No! I can guess what the doctor's telling them,"

Peg said, "but it's not true. You're going to get well. You have to!"

Danny swallowed hard and tried to moisten his lips with his tongue.

Peg supported his head and held a glass of water to his lips.

He took only a sip of water before he lay back against the pillow. His voice was weak as he said, "Remember when I told you that when I'm sixteen I'd join the Union Army and make Mike proud of me. I'm a good shot already, Peg."

"I know you are!" she said. She leaned closer, in her eagerness gripping his hand more tightly. "And in the meantime you've got school and friends and—"

"I won't make it to sixteen. I'm going to die, Peg."

"No! Don't say that!"

Tears welled up in his eyes and rolled down his cheeks. "I won't be able to do anything to make Mike proud of me. I'm going to die before I can do one single thing to help my country."

"Danny, that's not true!" Peg rubbed her own tears away with the back of one sleeve. "You saved my life today," she said. "And you may have saved the lives of many Union soldiers."

As Danny looked at her in bewilderment, Peg hurried to tell him what Miss Hennessey had confided about breaking the siege of Chattanooga. "When they learn of the Confederates' weakness, Grant's forces can take Chattanooga from the Rebs, Danny, and it will be an important Union victory. Miss Hennessey will get the information to General Grant, because you helped her."

"Peg," he whispered. "Is it really true?"

"It's true," she answered.

"I wish I could tell Mike."

"I'll write and tell him, Danny, after the battle takes place. I'll tell him it was won because of you. He'll be so proud of you!"

The pressure of Danny's fingers was gentle, and a smile flickered on his lips. "And of you, Peg. For a snoopy little sister, you're not so bad."

"Danny—"

"I'm tired, Peg," he said. "I'm going to sleep for a while."

As Danny closed his eyes, the smile still on his lips, Peg put her head down on the quilt and sobbed. "Don't leave me, Danny! Please don't go! I love you best, and I can't lose you! I can't!"

But Danny didn't answer.

Ma, whose voice was husky with sorrow, came in and sat beside her. "You need some rest, love. I'll be here with Danny," she said.

But Peg wouldn't let go of Danny's hand. Later— much later—she fell asleep, her fingers still intertwined with his.

In her dreams she heard sobbing—Ma and Ennie, even Alfrid—and Ma saying, "It's over. He's gone."

"Not yet," Peg wanted to tell them. "Not until after the battle and the Union victory, because Danny will have a part in it."

In late November broadsheets with news of General Grant's great Union victory at Chattanooga were printed and posted on walls and boarded-up windows throughout St. Joseph.

As she had promised, Peg wrote to Mike—and Frances and Megan. She described what she had read about the siege of Chattanooga that had caused great damage to Union troops and rail shipments, and bragged that Danny had played a part in helping General Grant's army to break that siege. She explained that she would be able to tell them the whole story as soon as the war had ended.

And she visited Danny's grave in the St. Joseph cemetery, where his body had been buried. It was wintery cold. The trees were twisted, black skeletons, and a heavy freeze had browned the grass. Peg had bought a small Union flag at Katherine Banks's store, but before she drove the thin pole into the earth in front of Danny's headstone she stopped, noting a dark shimmer of something lying near the headstone.

Peg picked up the familiar, obsidian arrowhead that she recognized as Marcus's lucky treasure, and tears burned her eyes. "You were a hero to all of us, Danny," she said. "A real Union hero."

As Grandma closed the journal, Jennifer wiped tears from her eyes. "No more stories about the war," she begged. "Oh, Grandma, I can't bear it!"

Grandma patted Jennifer's hand. "I can assure you there are no more stories of war in Frances Mary's journal. It's what happened *after* the war with some of Quantrill's raiders that Frances wrote about next."

"Wait a minute. If the war was over, wouldn't the raiders go home?" Jeff asked.

"I'm afraid not all of them wanted to," Grandma said. "Some of the men who had ridden with Quantrill and his lieutenant, Bloody Bill Anderson, couldn't give up their guerrilla ways. They became notorious and dangerous outlaws who held up trains, robbed banks, and terrorized the West. For instance, there were Cole and Jim Younger, Frank and Jesse James—"

Jeff jumped out of his chair. "Grandma! I know about those guys. I've read about them and seen stories about them in Western movies!" He stopped, his eyes wide. "Did any of the Kellys meet up with them?"

"It so happens," Grandma said, "that on one very frightening day one of the Kelly girls—"

But she broke off and stood up. "I'm getting ahead of myself," she said. "What happened on the Kansas plains is a story for another day."

"Grandma!" Jennifer complained.

"Which I'll tell you tomorrow," Grandma said. "I promise."

About the Author

JOAN LOWERY NIXON is the acclaimed author of more than a hundred books for young readers. She has served as regional vice-president for the Southwest Chapter of the Mystery Writers of America and is the only four-time winner of the Edgar Allan Poe Best Juvenile Mystery Award given by that society. She is also a two-time winner of the Western Writers of America's Golden Spur Award, which she won for *A Family Apart* and *In the Face of Danger,* the first and third books of the Orphan Train Adventures. She was moved by the true experiences of the children on the nineteenth-century orphan trains to research and write the Orphan Train Adventures, which also include *Caught in the Act, A Place to Belong,* and *A Dangerous Promise.*

Joan Lowery Nixon and her husband live in Houston.